I really liked *Vision*. I picked it up and finished it in a day, caught up in the action and richness of the plot. But *Vision* is much more than an ordinary thriller. Having been a consultant on the original remote viewing research, with enough security clearances to know the details of some of the operational remote viewing done for various US intelligence agencies, I was even more impressed. Schwartz was one of the pioneers in developing remote viewing, and in the form of an exciting novel he describes how this line of research developed, and how it can be used as well as, perhaps, connect us to Spirit more directly than the too often fossilized religions of today.

Charles Tart, PhD
Pioneer Parapsychological Researcher
Author of: *Altered States of Consciousness*

What if counter-terrorism experts at the Pentagon discovered a plot to explode a nuclear bomb in the United States, but they had no idea when or where? And what if a team of remote viewers accidentally foresaw that disaster, but they didn't know what to do with that information? *The Vision* is a fast-paced thriller that follows this scenario to its shocking conclusion. The author is a founder of modern remote viewing techniques, and the story is a fictionalized account of true, formerly classified psychic espionage missions.

Dean Radin, PhD.
Chief Scientist, Institute of Noetic Sciences
Author of: *Real Magic*

In *The Vision* Stephan Schwartz has created a suspenseful, well-crafted novel that explores the mysteries of human consciousness and poses vital issues that are imminent to address to ensure the survival of humanity. Stephan is a master teacher, who I will continue to learn from during my entire lifetime. Highly recommended!

Judith Orloff, MD
Author of: *Second Sight*

The Vision

A Novel of Time and Consciousness

STEPHAN A. SCHWARTZ

Greenwood Press
Langley, Washington

Greenwood Press
P.O. Box 905
Langley, Washington 98260
www.greenwoodpress.net

L.C. Cat. No.: 1-6488017981

ISBN: 978-0-9768536-6-4

This book was typeset in Baskerville.

Correspondence: To send correspondence to the author:
saschwartz@schwartzreport.net

Other Books by Stephan A. Schwartz

Non-fiction
The 8 Laws of Change
Opening to the Infinite
The Alexandria Project
The Secret Vaults of Time

Fiction
Awakening

In Memory of
Hella
George
Ingo
Alan
Jack
Michael
Terry
Fran

Who shared my adventures in consciousness, and who have moved on to an even greater adventure.

CHAPTER ONE

7 August – Moscow –

The venerable Metropol Hotel's elegant Tsarist lobby was crowded with people that early August mid-afternoon. Beneath the striking gilded bronze and crystal chandeliers, elegantly dressed men and women moved with purpose. Down the hall off the lobby, in front of one of the meeting rooms, a sign in an ornate brass frame read, "International Society of Physicians – Protocol Committee." Inside a group of doctors of many races and ethnicities sat around a large conference table talking over each other, their voices rising and falling in intensity as they debated in heavily accented English, the common language of science.

"I think we must assume that the World Health Organization is going to..." a spade-bearded olive-complected man made his point, as much with his hands as his words, which were interrupted in any case.

"I don't think we can assume anything of the kind, Dr Kaparatis. It clearly ...." a Norwegian doctor as solid as a block interjected, only to be himself interrupted.

"I have discussed this with Herr Professor Schmidt, and he completely concurs that our position on the vaccine is the proper one...." A third physician spoke up expressing his disdain in a heavy French accent, while looking at Kaparatis.

"Gentlemen," the chairman raised his voice to override them all. While this was getting sorted out, there was a knock on the door. An aide sitting near the entrance got up, opened it, listened for a moment, then turned and walked over to a handsome man in his thirties, obviously from the Middle East. On his suit jacket was pinned a plastic name plate, DR. DAOUD ABOU MABROOK. The aide leaned over to speak quietly in Mabrook's ear, "I'm sorry, doctor, there is someone … a man … he says it's urgent."

Mabrook was not startled; he seemed to have expected what he was being told. Without a word he got up, made an excusing gesture, and left the conference room following the young aide who led him down the corridor through the marble lobby into a glorious dining room with a colored glass conservatory ceiling two stories above the tables.

He was nervous as he looked around the room. A thumb drive had given him a picture of the man he was to meet, but it was the first time in all his travels that he was doing something he knew to be, in some way that he didn't understand but felt, surreptitious. He had agreed to the meeting when it was explained the option was damage to his sister's shop, upon which sixteen of his family members depended.

Finally he saw his man seated at a table next to one of the brown marble pillars that lined the room's sides. He was a small badly-shaven elderly man in an ill-fitting green suit. He had thick glasses held together by scotch tape, and looked very out of place amidst the couture-dressed women and their bespoke-tailored men.

Seeing him, the doctor looked quizzically at the aide. The picture he had been given was a headshot showing only the face without the glasses, like a passport photo, giving no hint as to his general appearance. This individual was not at all what had expected, and it threw him off balance. The elderly man in contrast seemed quite comfortable to be there and to have Mabrook coming over toward him. Before they got to the table the aide leaned in, saying softly, "Do not let his appearance deceive you, doctor. Alexander Leonovich is very powerful. He handles certain matters for Putin, he is a serious man. We all know that."

As they approached, the elderly man stood up and extended his hand. "Alexander Leonovich Vorontsov, a pleasure to meet you, Dr. Mabrook." After a pause he gestured to the table, "Please join me."

Mabrook took the final step to the table and sat down. As soon as he did the waiter came over and handed both men menus.

"I cannot be away that long," Mabrook said, waving the menu away. From a distance it all looked very ordinary, but Mabrook felt a deep tension, as if he were being watched by a cobra.

"Perhaps just some tea, then. I'll have some myself," Vorontsov said, sitting down.

Mabrook nodded his agreement and the waiter left, as did the aide. As soon as they were out of earshot Mabrook began to speak without preamble.

"You know I do not ordinarily do this. I'm not quite sure what to say. The news is good?" he asked as he looked at Vorontsov, who returned his attention with a quiet smile. Tilting his head he looked at the younger man through his thick glasses.

"We have been very fortunate. Turkmenistan is ... confused. Recent developments .... The package you are inquiring about is going to be ... misplaced. Happily, thanks to your organization's generosity, we will be the ones to find it. You understand?"

"When."

"I think within the week."

The waiter approached with the tea and served both men. As they took up their cups the tension relaxed. Their business was complete. Mabrook was glad it had been simple, and all he had to do was make a routine call to his sister.

CHAPTER TWO

12 August — Ashkhabad, Turkmenistan —

Five days later as business was ending, at an industrial installation outside of Ashgabat, Turkmenistan, two men in dark green jumpsuits were loading a truck with military green containers and barrels. Standing next to them in blue jumpers were the driver and his assistant. Everything seemed normal, yet the expressions on the faces of all the men made it clear it was not an ordinary day; everyone was on edge. As the last container moved up the ramp it almost fell off the handcart. Revealed on its side was the international nuclear symbol. The two plant men became very agitated as the container rocked on its dolly, as did the driver and his assistant. They rushed forward, and got it stabilized and into the two-and-a-half ton truck without further incident.

Once the plant men had everything on board and secured, the senior one handed a clipboard with the paperwork to the trucker who signed it and handed it back. The plant man tore off a copy and returned it to driver. As soon as he had the paperwork in his hands the driver and his assistant climbed into their truck, started it up, and pulled away, driving past the military guard post at the chain link fence.

Two days and eight hundred miles later, late at night near the Iran border, the truck pulled over onto the shoulder of the isolated highway curving around a bay. The driver and his assistant turned off the engine and got out. The assistant walked into the scrubby landscape to take a leak and was just coming back when another two-and-a-half ton truck came up the road. It pulled past them and backed up so that the two trucks were back to back. Two men in their twenties got out speaking Farsi. Through their truck's open doors the cab, lit only by the glow from the instrument panel, revealed an interior decorated with garish colors. The plaintive wail of Islamic music coming out of the truck's speakers filled the air.

Almost without a word the four men moved the container with the nuclear symbol from one truck to another. Then each truck turned and drove back the way it had come.

In the new truck the men shared a water bottle and settled in for the long drive back to the coastal town of Bandar Torkaman, Iran. Several hours into the drive they came up a hill and around a curve and saw an accident in front of them. One truck was aflame. It was a common road scene, and at first they thought nothing of it. Trucks drove without their lights, a hangover from war. Things happened.

The driver slowed to a stop, and as he did so a team of men, faces covered by traditional Islamic head scarves, leapt onto the truck's running boards and garroted the two men in the cab. A pickup truck drove up, and the two killers and the truck driver off-loaded the nuclear container into the smaller truck. When that was completed, the original truck with the two dead bodies was rigged to drive full speed into the two already wrecked vehicles ahead. As it smashed into the pile-up, it also burst into flames, and the burning trucks lit up the night sky. The fire was reflected in the rearview mirror as one of the men in the truck now carrying the nuclear material unwrapped his head cloth revealing his face, which was Korean.

The truck crossed back into Turkmenistan and raced for the coast of the Caspian Sea. At the village of Serdar it turned left down an even smaller road, arriving at the coast a few hours later. There was nothing to see but sand, some driftwood, and waves. In spite of that the driver stopped, pulled off the road, parked and waited. Within an hour a small coastal freighter came into view. It stopped and lowered the ship's tender, a dirty white open boat that came to shore and gently grounded on the beach as the truck moved forward to the water's edge to meet it. Leaving one man with the boat, the three other crewmen who had made the crossing and the men from the truck opened the back of the pickup and slung the container with the nuclear symbol onto a web of canvas straps, and manhandled it out to the boat.

It took all of them to push the boat off the beach. When it was floating freely again the seamen got back in, turned on the engine and reversed out a hundred yards, then turned and steered to the freighter. By the time it got there the ship had lowered its boom cable with a cargo net. They maneuvered the container into the net and hoisted it aboard. Then they lifted the boat. On the beach the truck was already gone.

CHAPTER THREE

14 September — Libyan Desert —

A small barrel-chested heavily-bearded bald man, Basma El Farouk leaned over a toy train with intense concentration. Everything about him was very precise. The small machine was clearly hand made and a jewel of miniaturization. Slowly and carefully, looking through a magnifying glass, he fitted a final piece into place. There was a kind of leashed calm about him as he did this. Overhead the drone of a plane could be heard. Farouk took note of the sound and carefully put the small train engine back into the fitted foam compartment of an aluminum case and replaced his tools with equal deliberation.

He reached into his shirt and pulled out a lanyard, on the end of which was a ring of keys. He took the ring off the lanyard, selected a small key, locked the case, put the ring back on the lanyard, dropped it back inside his shirt, turned out the light and left the room, walking out of the converted forty-foot steel cargo container into the glaring sunlight of the desert. Other containers, all painted in camouflage desert tan, were clustered around the one he had just exited. On the hard desert floor to one side groups of men were engaged in training exercises: some were shooting at human shaped targets whose faces were those of Western leaders, others were running an obstacle course, still others sat on folding chairs under a camouflage canvas open-sided pavilion learning how to make suicide vests.

Farouk looked up, shielded his eyes, and watched a small twin engine plane land on a beaten earth airstrip a hundred yards off. As soon as its engines were cut, men rushed forward and off-loaded the container with the nuclear warning symbol, as well as some other supplies. The off-loading was directed by a younger bearded man, speaking Arabic. As Farouk walked up to where he was standing the man stopped speaking and deferentially turned to Farouk, who gestured for him to continue.

"Be careful. Or you'll be in pieces smaller than a sand flea," the young man said to the men trying to get the container out of the plane.

"Don't worry, Sameer," Farouk said, quietly, "Until it is armed you've nothing to fear. Safe as a baby and not as much trouble. Have them take it to the lab."

The plane, freed of its cargo, started up again and began taxiing to take off. A pickup truck drove up to where the men with the container were standing and they loaded the container into its open back end. The truck drove just a few hundred yards to a metal barn-like structure bigger than the shipping containers but painted in the same colors. One of the men got out and pushed back the sliding doors, then went back to help the others bring the container into the building. Within the interior there was a smaller space defined by clear plastic sheeting walls to keep the desert dust out, and inside the enclosure two men in white protective technical suits were carrying out some kind of operation.

Farouk and Sameer walked into the building, passing through the outer plastic walls into a kind of foyer space where they put on white technical suits and slipped booties over their shoes, then passed through into the inner space. The building's sliding door was closed, reducing the glaring light of the desert to the more tolerable level of electric lighting hanging down from the ceiling. Air conditioners hummed and a generator could be heard in the background. Two men brought the container into the outer space and left. Farouk, assisted by Sameer, used a little rolling electric crane to pick up the container and place it on a trolley which they wheeled into the walled-off inner room, where they opened it. Inside, nestled in foam, was a dull silvery metal cylinder with a spherical end. With the little crane they lifted the whole assemblage onto a stainless steel table. With Zen-like calm, Farouk took up a tool and began to open the cylinder and very deliberately take it apart.

CHAPTER FOUR

14 September — London —

Nancy Templeton, an elegant middle-aged woman, was the serving American Deputy Chief of Station and Coordinator of Intelligence in London, and was already having a bad day when Jason Bernstein, her opposite number in Operations, came into her office at the American Embassy.

"Good afternoon, Nancy," Bernstein said as he entered. He was a man in his late thirties with an almost military-style haircut and a government managementlevel dark suit.

"You look particularly grim this morning, Jason what now?" Templeton asked, looking up from her computer and brushing her stylishly cut dark hair out of her face.

"This just came in from Langley," he responded, handing her the cable print-out he was holding. Templeton read it and her expression radically changed.

"Jason, a five kiloton theater nuclear warhead is loose in the international terrorist network, and there are several groups working together. God. Does anyone have any idea where it's headed?"

"The Brits think there's an ISIL connection, but that the Russians are somehow in the mix, as are the Iranians and North Koreans, can you believe it? But what really has them exercised is they are concerned it may be headed here for some local self-activated terror group in the city. You know, some group made up of apparently ordinary native-born citizens we've never heard of."

"The nightmare," Templeton responded.

"The nightmare, yes. We could be talking about taking London out," Bernstein said, sinking into the arm chair near Templeton's desk.

"Does the Prime Minister know yet?"

"Max is meeting with her as we speak."

"It's really going to happen," Templeton said, looking with great earnestness at Bernstein.

"Killing a million of us in a heart beat... yeah."

"Do we have any idea how it might come in? What the timing is?"

"As of half an hour ago both MI-5 and MI-6 are totally focused on it. So is everyone in the U.S. They are buttoning everything up. But..." Bernstein made a face, "there is some evidence something unplanned went on. We think the device was stolen when that installation in Turkmenistan was closing down a month ago. We have some evidence that the group that stole it were, themselves, hijacked. I went back through the file and saw some reports of a wreck involving the truck that was carrying it down near the Iranian border."

"Some kind of intra-movement struggle?" Templeton asked, coming around from her desk to sit in the chair across from Bernstein.

"Yes. But exactly who or why we haven't a clue."

"Jesus, Jason. This is all getting very scary. It really is endless war."

"Yeah. Listen, I just wanted to let you know. We're going to put everything we can together and hold a briefing at fourteen hundred in the SKIF."

"Alright. Let me pulse my net. I'll let you know... Five kilotons. Do you think I should get my daughter out of the city?"

"I'm telling Janet to take ours and herself up to the Lake District. I figure that's probably the safest place in the country."

"Could she take Lily and her nanny? The kids know each other."

"Sure, I'll have Janet contact her school."

"Here. Let me give you a note," Templeton said, taking a piece of her note stationery, writing out a sentence, then handing it to Bernstein. "Thanks, I really appreciate this."

CHAPTER FIVE

16 September — Washington, D.C. —

The leaves were just beginning to turn in Georgetown, an 18th century town on the Potomac now part of the District of Columbia, and one of the city's most fashionable neighborhoods. Its mix of federal and Victorian architecture and brick sidewalks gave it a village character unique in the city. A green Volvo station wagon driven by an attractive woman in her early thirties pulled up in front of a red brick Roman Catholic girl's school. In the back seat was her daughter, a girl about seven. Tracy Walsh got out of the car and went around to open the door to let Sarah out and help her maneuver a papier maché elephant painted with childish care. The little girl was dressed in a blue skirt and sweater with a white blouse, the school uniform. Other similarly dressed girls of varying ages were on the street and going up the granite steps to the school.

"Careful, Mommy. His nose will break."

"We'll we wouldn't want that to happen, not after you worked so hard. But how do you know it's a he, Sarah?"

"It's Barbar," the child answered, as if talking to a child. "Everyone knows he's a he... a boy, Mommy." Barely able to hold the elephant, the little girl started up the stairs, then turned back around with a serious look on her face. "I never get to be with you and Daddy together anymore. Does divorce mean we'll never do things all together again?"

Tracy went over and knelt in front of her child so they were eye to eye. "We'll do things together again. But not quite yet. I don't think Daddy's ready for that."

The little girl started to tear up. "Divorce isn't fair. Why don't you both just say you're sorry and make up the way you tell me to do with my friends?"

"We are sorry, sweetheart. Daddy and I are very sorry that we can't be happy living together. But remember. . . we are very happy about one thing."

"What?"

"You. We're very happy about you. Now take Barbar in and show 'em what a great elephant he is." She hugged her daughter who was hugging the elephant, and the little girl turned and began awkwardly climbing the steps.

Just before she got to the landing Sarah looked back at her mother who was watching her and said, "Oh, I will. Jenny Carter is going to be so jealous. She made an elephant too, but his nose broke." Another child went over to Sarah and said something, and they climbed the last few steps and were soon lost in the crowd pouring through the doors. Over the arch of the entrance was a statue of the Virgin Mary, and carved into the granite plinth, "Immaculate Heart Preparatory."

Tracy returned to her car, drove a short distance up the street and turned left onto the grounds of Georgetown University into the area labeled "Faculty Only," where she parked. She reached back, grabbed her briefcase, got out and began walking across the green campus lawn studded with old trees and surrounded by 19th century gothic collegiate stone buildings, one of which she entered. Inside, the corridors were filled with college students, some of whom acknowledged her, and she smiled at them or waved back. She went down the hall to a classroom and went in. Students followed her; many others were already seated in the tiers above the lecture floor. It was obviously a popular class. The high-ceilinged old-fashioned room was bright with the early fall light that poured through the tall windows. Tracy went over to the lecturer's desk, took out her tablet which she hooked into the AV system, and turned to face rows and rows of students. As she did so the room quieted and she began.

"The neurophysiological components of the shamanic trance state are complex. However, they invariably are composed of certain common ritual elements, regardless of the culture. Drumming. Chanting. Collectively making a statement of intention. All play their role."

An hour later, just as the class was ending, an African-American woman in her mid-thirties entered at the back of the room and caught Tracy's eye. She acknowledged her presence, tipping her head slightly, and wrapped up the class with, "Okay people. Tomorrow we'll finish this. Let me remind you that your papers on contemporary American rituals are due Thursday, and I expect you all to have read Stanley Krippner's paper on the role of altered states in Amazonian rituals by next class and come prepared to talk about it."

Just as she finished the bell rang, and the students picked up their gear and exited, talking amongst themselves. As the room cleared the woman who came in at the end walked down the tiers to where Tracy was standing.

"God, the thundering herd. How about lunch at 1789?"

"You're on. Let's walk; there's never any place to park on 36th."

The two women walked out of the building down the tree-lined drive and out of the campus' pillared gates.

"How's it going?"

"Oh God, Nina, I don't know. I didn't want this. Keith knows that," Tracy said, and stopped to wipe her eyes before continuing, "Sarah said this morning that divorce isn't fair. I didn't know what to say."

"What's not fair is a husband who's jealous of his wife's career success, and who's behaving like a real bastard. That's what's not fair."

"It's hard for him, Nina. He should have married a woman who stayed inside the picket fence instead of one going off to study tribes and their rituals."

"What did he expect when he married a field anthropologist?"

"Keith didn't really seem to mind until the Richardson Award. Even the two hundred and fifty thousand dollars that came with it didn't take out the sting. Actually, in some ways I think it made it worse. So I guess my success has screwed my family life. How do you do it? You're off to your archaeological digs in Africa for months at a time. How does that work?"

"You're a good mother, Tracy. You've tried to be a supportive wife and you've still managed to write two books, win fellowships from Guggenheim, Ford ... damn near every major foundation in the country... and now the Richardson. Why do you keep apologizing? Keith doesn't have your chops. He knows it. End of story. As for me, Charley's as involved with his work at CERN as I am with mine. We try to work it out to both be away at the same time, so I don't think he even notices," Nina said, then gave a knowing smile. "But it's very hot when we're together."

The women got to the restored 18th century building that housed the 1789 restaurant, and were led to a table by the maitre d'. They looked around at the elegant room with its large fireplace, beamed ceilings, and 18th and 19th century prints, then turned to the menus the maitre d' handed them.

"Your waiter will be with you in a moment. May I tell him what you would like to drink?"

"House cab for me, what about you Tracy?"

"I'll have that wonderful Sauvignon Blanc you served me last time, Michael."

"Very good," the man responded, and walked away, leaving the women to look at their menus.

"I'm having the flounder. I had it here the other day and it was great."

"The lamb chops for me."

The waiter came over to serve them their wine and take their orders; he turned out to be one of Nina's graduate students.

"Hello professors, what can I get you?

They placed their orders and he left. For a moment they sat in silence, drinking their wine, then Nina broke the silence.

"I think there is more to it than that, Tracy. You told me there were religious issues as well."

"I may not go to church anymore, and I'm afraid I'm no longer a believing Catholic, not since that pedophile thing… you remember … but divorce isn't … I never saw this in my future, Nina."

"Who on earth ever sees their own future, Tracy?"

"That reminds me," Tracy responded, brightening. "Change of subject. I'm trying to learn more about religious trance rituals. Like speaking in tongues and prophecy. Do you know a professor here, Michael Gillespie?"

"The spook neurology professor? All that psychic woo woo stuff? What in the world has he..."

The waiter returned with their orders and for a few moments the two women focused on eating. Then Tracy picked up the thread.

"I did a literature review, and Gillespie's written some very impressive stuff on altered states of consciousness. What do you know about him?"

"Met him at a faculty function once. He knew something about my work, so of course I thought he was brilliant; how many White neuroscientists know anything about the archaeology of the 12 churches of Lalibela in Ethiopia?" Nina said with a laugh. "Whatever he's doing it seems a little weird but reasonably well funded, which, as we both know, covers a multitude of sins. Why do you ask?"

"I'm trying to learn more about religious trance rituals."

The women finished their lunch, and as they did, Tracy looked at her watch and signaled the waiter, handing him her credit card.

"This one's on me, Nina; you've been a wonderful friend, and I really thank you. I'm sorry to rush like this, but I have an appointment with Dr. Gillespie in 15 minutes." As she finished the waiter returned, she signed the slip and got up to leave. Nina got up as well and the two women threaded their way through the tables and out onto the street.

They hugged, and as Tracy turned to leave Nina said with a small leer, "Did I mention he's good looking too?"

They both laughed and went their separate ways. Tracy walked quickly back toward the campus but stopped short of it in front of a large grey stone Victorian house one block over from her daughter's school. The house had a turret with a conical roof like a witch's hat. A brass plaque screwed to the wall next to its front door read, LYNN HILL HUMAN CAPACITIES INSTITUTE. At the top of a short flight of stone stairs was a vaulted entrance with a recessed black door. A ramp went down under the stairs to a lower entrance. Tracy hesitated, reassessing what she was about to do, nodded her head slightly "yes" reflexively, then mounted the stairs. She rang the bell and a young woman, clearly a student, answered.

"I'm Professor Walsh. I have an appointment with Professor Gillespie."

"Come on in. I'll tell Michael you're here."

Inside, the house was light and airy, not at all weird. Several young graduate students were working in a room off the hall, doing something on computers. On the walls there were odd combinations of what looked like doodles or childish drawings and photographs, one of each in the same frame. As Tracy was looking at these a tall blond-haired man, about thirty-five, wearing a flannel shirt, tweed coat, and blue jeans, came up behind her without her noticing.

"The drawings are the participant's impressions... we call it remote viewing... and the photographs are the targets the remote viewers were trying to perceive."

Tracy looked again at the framed images. "They're uncanny. Really the... what did you call them, remote viewers... know nothing about the target? What instructions are they given?"

"Usually the target doesn't even exist as a designated target at the time the session data is collected. In this case though," indicating the drawing made by the viewer and the target picture of a waterfall surrounded by forest that looked much the same as the drawing, "the viewer was given a sealed opaque envelope that contained a microdot about the size of a period at the end of a sentence in a book, which was glued to a 3 by 5 card. The microdot contained an image not of the target itself but just the numbers of the latitude and longitude of the target. The viewer was asked to describe what they perceived there."

"Are you serious?" Tracy asked in disbelief.

"Yes, quite. It's a standard protocol." Turning to face her he smiled and said, "I'm Michael Gillespie, and you must be my two-thirty appointment, Tracy Walsh. Let's go up to my office." He led the way up stairs lighted from above by a skylight. When they got to the next floor he led her down a short hall into what was obviously once the master bedroom suite. His office was filled with books and papers, two brown leather club chairs and a leather couch. At his workstation there were three computer screens.

Michael gestured to a chair. Tracy sat down, and he joined her in a chair across the coffee table. French doors were open to a wrought iron balcony that overlooked a garden at the back of the house.

"You said you were interested in my work on altered states?"

"As I said, I'm an anthropologist."

"Of course you are. Your paper on the Ubanda tribe's healing rituals in the *American Anthropologist* was great. Although I think they are more aware of the physiological processes they invoke than you seem to believe."

"You've read it?"

"I've read a number of your things. How could I not? You're one of the few people who think it isn't all sleight-of-hand and manipulation by the shaman to maintain his power and tribal status. Your last paper seemed to suggest you even believe something real is going on, even if we don't know the mechanism. Am I right?"

"There has to be," Tracy answered with emphasis. "These rituals wouldn't survive from one generation to the next over centuries unless something real was happening. These people aren't stupid, they just have a different world view. It isn't just tribal power politics."

"I agree . . . but we are a minority," Michael said. "Can I get you something... tea...coffee... Apollinaris water?"

"No thank you, I just had lunch. But who cares we're a minority? Something's either right or it's not. Listen, I've got a problem and I need your help. I've been lucky enough to be selected for a Richardson..."

"I heard. Congratulations, Tracy. You can do something really worthwhile with that much money. What are you going to do with the funding?"

"For three years I've been trying to set up an extended visit with a tribe in the upper Brazilian Amazon called the Yconda. People who've gone up river report they enter a trance state that allows them to communicate over long distances... I don't know... mentally... psychically... something... with a tribe they claim to guide and protect. It all sounded like myth content until Dunne at Pittsburgh found a tribe in Ecuador that reported their elders help them by impressing images on their minds, which their shaman interprets." Tracy said, pulling over her briefcase.

As she searched through it she looked up at Michael. "I found both papers and compared the images. The drawings they made... the images they said the elders were sending them ...they're exactly like those drawn by Yconda shamans when they enter the 'speaking trance' as they call it." The words spilled out of Tracy, and as she looked into Michael's face she saw he really understood them in the way she wanted to learn, and there was more.

"You'll see it, it's easy to spot," she said, and pulled her tablet from her briefcase and laid it on the coffee table. It showed the two tribal images, and they were oddly similar to the framed remote viewing targets and session data in the hallway below.

"Fascinating. Could I copy these?"

"That's the charm, Michael," Tracy said with growing excitement. "This is all in the open literature, just different disciplines, different journals. I'll send you the URLs," she said, tapping on her tablet. "Nobody had made the connection before, but it was very clear to me. "

"I get it. This is nonlocal perception just in a different cultural context, Tracy."

"Exactly," Tracy said with excitement in her voice. "When I searched Academia and PubMed, your published reports on what you call Remote Viewing were the closest things I could find to the Yconda experience. If I'm going to study this properly, it would help if I knew more about how this works."

"When do you go?"

"Next spring. No specific date. But I have to be up river before the end of summer, or I can't get all the way up. So please tell me about remote viewing."

"The best way for you to understand remote viewing is for you to do it. Then you can read and really comprehend the literature, and there is a lot of it by the way. The thing about altered states is you have to experience them to understand them."

"You mean, do it?"

"In my terms it's a protocol, in yours a ritual. A way of allowing yourself to open to an aspect of consciousness we call nonlocal because it is not physiologically based. The only way to really understand what you want to know is to directly experience the process."

"Okay. I can't argue with that," Tracy replied, and for a moment their eyes connected. "What do I do?"

"Most anyone can remote view. In the old days it used to be called clairvoyance. There's nothing supernatural about it. Sorry, no ghosts, goblins, or cherubim. It's a normal human ability, like playing a musical instrument. Some people are better at it than others, of course, just as some are better violin players or skiers. Though most of us can learn enough to play a tune, or get down a hill."

"What if I'm tone deaf?" Tracy replied, revealing her nervousness.

"I will predict you are not," Michael said, very matter of fact. It made Tracy wonder what it was he saw in her. As if reading her thoughts, Michael said with no preamble, "You're a cultural anthropologist. You are interested in ritual consciousness. It wasn't hard," he said with a smile.

He turned to his Echo, and said, "Karen" who, after a beat, came online. "Is anyone in the session room?"

"No, Michael, it's open."

"Well, get it queued up, will you please? I'm coming down."

CHAPTER SIX

16 September — Washington, D.C. —

Michael led Tracy down a back set of stairs into a pantry that opened to what must once have been the high-ceilinged dining room. The room had white wooden wainscoted walls with ivory-colored plaster up to the prominent crown molding. In the middle of the room there was what looked like a giant egg, a curved structure about ten feet high and eight feet around. It had a low sheen, and its color matched the walls.

Noticing her looking at the structure, Michael said, "We call it the egg. When you are dealing with consciousness, aesthetics are important. They modify sense impressions." Walking over to the egg he added, "It's a Faraday cage, so it's shielded on the inside from electromagnetic radiation. Your phone won't work in there. And you will not be bombarded with all the electromagnetic radiation we normally live with. It's also sound-proofed, with purified air and constant temperature and humidity." He pressed on the egg and a door panel appeared which he opened, revealing a soft gray room with pleated cloth-covered walls, indirect light, and not a single right angle. He led her into this strange tapered space containing two large soft leather chairs the same color as the walls. Over the chairs hung a kind of helmet. Michael gestured for Tracy to sit in one of the chairs, and he sat in the other.

"What a strange room. There are no corners, no colors, nothing to focus your eyes on, yet it is very calming and intimate. In my terms you've created the temple," Tracy said as she looked around.

"Exactly. Empirical science, passing observations down from one generation to the next, yields many useful insights. That's why I study shamanism and how I came across your work. The religious aspect of sacred space is entirely denominational and human-defined. But across all the belief systems, no matter the geography or culture, there are certain common characteristics to spaces where opening to nonlocal consciousness is the goal. We're looking for inner-vision, and this space incorporates everything we know from both objective research and empirical science about optimizing the process," Michael said as he looked down at the arm of his chair. He pushed a button and an arm with a tray swung around with a tablet on it. He punched something in, then looked at Tracy and said, "You can adjust your seat. Make yourself as comfortable as you can."

As she did this, he added, "You don't have to have all this. I've seen people do successful remote viewings on a pitching ship, when they had to vomit over the side in the middle of doing their session before they could go on. And in a one hundred and twenty-degree desert with the mid-day sun shining down. But the egg optimizes conditions for opening to nonlocal consciousness. Anthropologically you might think of it as a modern temple of Aesculapius roughly similar in purpose to the ancient temple at Epidaurus in Greece…"

"Where people went to have dreams which the Therapeutae interpreted."

"Yes, exactly."

"Thanks. I thought that was probably the case, and was going to ask you after the session. I appreciate you telling me."

Michael adjusted the lighting until it was diffused and dim, like a porch at twilight in the summer, and keyed his tablet. The room was very silent, and then a soft tone, barely heard, filled the room like a scent. Anticipating Tracy's question he said, "C to G (fifth) slightly sharp. The work of a musicologist named Harold Grandstaff Moses. It helps prepare the mind for the experience."

Michael reached up and pulled down the soft helmet and put it on.

"Could you do this as well, Tracy? We record a full biometric profile of both the monitor and the viewer during the session."

"Wow," Tracy said, and pulled the helmet down over her head. It was very comfortable, almost pleasant, and it helped her relax.

Michael keyed his tablet, "This is session 426," glancing down at a read out. "Viewer is Tracy Walsh... T-R-A-C-Y W-A-L-S-H. Interviewer Michael Gillespie. Time and date code now," he said, pressing the tablet again.

"We make a complete record of everything that takes place during a session. Are you comfortable?"

"Yes. Very. I'm fascinated... I had no idea..."

"Fifteen minutes after this part of the session ends I will show you a target image. I will do this here in this room. Your target's a real place, somewhere on planet earth. I do not know the answer, the target image hasn't been selected yet, you cannot get this information from my mind. I cannot unconsciously cue you. Your job is to describe the locale in the image you will be shown, using your nonlocal awareness. You cannot achieve the answer through reasoning. Close your eyes...," he said, and Tracy did as he asked.

"Take three deep breaths. By the end of the third breath, your mind will be clear." Tracy did as he instructed and felt herself relaxing and becoming focused on being present.

"I want you to hold the intention that the image you will be shown appears in your mind. There will be a major geometric shape in the image; could you please draw that for me with the stylus on your tablet?"

Michael paused, and Tracy looked down at her tablet and with the stylus drew a shape. It appeared on Michael's tablet. Tracy had drawn a tall slender triangle.

"You are life-sized and you see the target location clearly. What do you see?

"A tall triangle. A tall metal triangle… how odd," Tracy answered. "This tall triangle is in a city that does not speak English. I know what this is… it's a radio tower."

"Don't analyze," Michael said. "Your intellect is trying to figure out how to make sense of what you're perceiving. That's how you make mistakes. Your task is just to get the images, the sense impressions. My job is to figure out what they mean."

"Well, it looks like a radio tower!" Tracy said with some asperity.

Not reacting at all, Michael asked, "Anything else? Experience the target with all your senses… touch, taste… just as you do in your normal waking state."

"There is a river in this city; I can smell the water. The air is polluted. I can smell that too. People go up inside of this triangle."

"What is your sense of the triangle's age?"

Tracy paused for a moment before speaking, "It's more than hundred years old. It was built… with some kind of ceremonial event in mind. That's all I get. I'm losing focus."

"You did fine," Michael said, then added, "Session ends now," and touched his tablet.

"It was so easy. A little like daydreaming. But what's the answer? You really don't know?"

"I really don't, Tracy. Right now there is no answer. There are fifteen hundred targets in the computer's memory. The target could be any one of them. At a random interval over the next 15 minutes the computer will randomly select one and then show it to us. The answer lies in the future. We have to wait. This is a triple blind protocol; there is no correct answer at the time you proffered the data."

"In critical ways it was very much like a shaman's journey. How in the world did you ever get into this?"

"How in the world did you get to be an anthropologist?"

"Your field is a little more unusual than mine. I was fascinated by other people's points of view."

"So was I," Michael responded, and they both laughed, recognizing there was an attraction between them. Suddenly a soft chime went off, and the room darkened.

"Time for the payoff. Here's the 'target'."

An image appeared on the opposite side of the egg. It was the Eiffel Tower with Paris spread out around it and the Seine flowing through it. Michael pressed a button on his tablet. Tracy's drawings appeared next to the target image. The accuracy of her inner vision was obvious and unequivocal even without her words, which had been transcribed and could be read in a third panel.

"Almost all of your observations were correct. The only place you went seriously wrong was with calling it a radio tower. That's where most people get into trouble until they learn to stop. It's called analytical overlay. You sense something and immediately try to put a label on it."

"Well, it still looks like a radio tower," Tracy said.

"Yes, it does," Michael admitted. "But it's not, and that difference is important."

CHAPTER SEVEN

Friday 27 September — Mallow, Ireland —

Three British SAS commandos in a Range Rover station wagon were driving late at night down the narrow roads of the Blackwater region of the Irish countryside. They were dressed in dark civilian clothes, sturdy very low key but well-designed outdoor wear. They all had short haircuts and were physically powerful. At a distance though, both they and the car were nondescript, as they were designed to be.

It was raining heavily with occasional lightning, and there was no moon. Stone walls and bramble hedgerows lined both sides of the country lane. Occasionally there was a break where one could see that houses, widely separated, lay beyond. All was dark.

The sergeant in the front passenger seat spoke over his shoulder to his captain who was sitting in the back; his accent was urban London.

"We've been watching for a week, sir. They smuggled it in almost certainly through Knockadoon Head. That's down in Youghal Bay."

"And what makes you think it has come to this patch, Bobby?" replied the captain, who was clearly in charge although his tone revealed there was a camaraderie independent of rank amongst these men. The officer spoke with a public school accent.

The driver, a corporal, lowest ranking of the three, demonstrated the men's closeness by speaking up in a thick North country accent. "Yah. Yoo know Bobby, surh. Not a man to go out without his belt and braces." The three of them shared the kind of private laugh only men who have faced real danger and relied upon one another can pull off.

The sergeant answered the question: "We've got a man in the local IRA cell. He says he was detailed to drive a metal case down here. There was a tag in Arabic, and it was delivered by an Asian. Japanese he thought, but maybe Korean. Everyone was on edge, so says our lad. He said it was a like a big metal footlocker. He never saw what was in it."

"My. Very nice that. Good work, Bobby."

The captain reached into what looked like a black gym bag and pulled out two very lightweight black nylon hooded rain anoraks, saying, "Her majesty doesn't want you wet now, Bobby. I've brought something for both of us."

He passed one to the sergeant, and then pulled out night goggles, two black flashlights with red lenses, and a tube of dark camouflage face paint.

The sergeant and the captain wrestled themselves into the slickers and started blacking their faces.

"Captain," the sergeant said as they were doing this, "Mick and I were over yesterday with a lady Mick met." He paused for the laughter. "Total innocent she was. Stopped down the road and watched. Bird watchers we were. Got a good look until a red Volkswagen from the caretaker's lodge showed up. Went right into 'Teachers on Holiday.' Didn't we Mick?"

"Maps and all. Daphne thought Bobby here taught shop to the kiddies."

"They chased us off, but before they did we could see the main house is deserted. Checked it out... the owner is an Italian... almost never in residence. Probably knows nothing about all this. That's the usual way. He's the cover... nothing nasty to show up in the records. It's the caretaker, of course. That means it's almost certainly in the big stone barn. Completely ordinary for him to go in and out of there."

"That's not all, suhr," Mick the corporal said. "These lads are too clever by half. They've got electrical cattle strips about ankle level at odd angles all over the fields, particularly near the barn. Y'ud never see'em from the road, and the placement makes no sense for animals. If you walk into one at night... well, it would hurt... an alarm somewhere would go off. Very effective. Must remember that one."

"We went back last night, bad luck for Mick with the lovely Daphne. No rain, thank God, and worked it out."

"Took Bobby all night while I sat crouched down in the bleeding car up the road."

"It's comin' up, Captain."

"The usual, Mick. Slow to twenty kilometers. With any luck we may be able to stop this scrim by stealing the ball," which drew another chuckle.

The car gently slowed.

The captain counting softly, "One ...two ...three...Now!"

The two men in unison opened the left side doors front and back. No light went on; it had been taped before they left. They rolled out and across the road to the hedge. Mick kept on moving through the whole exit. Even if the rain were not already drowning out all other noise, no one would hear a car stop.

They got up and brushed themselves off. The rain poured down, and it was very black. No stars, no moon. They put on their night goggles and checked their flashlights. Bobby led off through a break in the hedge. They moved in a careful high stepping motion, with starts, stops and turns. Bobby, the sergeant, was counting steps aloud, but so softly it could only be heard by the captain, who mimicked his every move. Bobby suddenly froze and in that instant lightning flashed, revealing a strip of electric fence lying right in front of them. They turned right. Bobby began counting again, and they worked their way closer to the barn.

They reached it just as another flash lit up its side, making the sliding door stand out and showing the location of the man door within it. Bobby moved to one side, the Captain to the other. They did not know whether anyone was inside. The captain took out a stethoscope, put it in his ears and the little trumpet against the door. After listening for a moment, he gestured to Bobby who reached for the door and slowly turned the knob. It was locked. The captain reached inside his slicker, pulled out a little kit and knelt in front of the door. Bobby leaned over him, shielding him from the rain.

The Captain pointed to his eyes and then the door, and Bobby flashed his red flashlight quickly, just enough to allow the captain to find the keyhole. It was a new lock. The seconds ticked by as the two men focused on the lock. At one point the Captain looked up and shook his head negatively, then took a breath and tried again. Suddenly the lock gave way. They moved back to either side of the door and Bobby slowly eased it open just a half-inch. No light came out and he quickly opened it wider. There was no response. With the agility of real athletes they moved through it, closing it behind them.

It was even darker in the barn than it was outside, so dark the goggles didn't work, and they turned them off. Bobby flicked his red flashlight on. The Captain clicked on his. By this limited light it appeared to be a barn, not for horses but for cattle. One side held a farm office and parking space for a tractor. They went through that quickly but methodically. Nothing unusual. On the other side was a large space filled to about ten feet with hay bales. Then there was a loft, and it was filled to the rafters with more bales. It looked exactly as one would expect an Irish cattle estate should look.

The men began working their way around the periphery and found nothing. They got to the wall of hay and spent a moment just looking at it. They exchanged a look and each pulled one end of a bale. It came out with difficulty. Behind it was a space like a room. But there was nothing immediately to be seen. They pulled out another bale, and the captain wriggled through, followed by Bobby.

They found themselves in a hidden space created by the stacked hay bales. It was empty. After checking the small space they turned to leave, and just as the captain bent to climb out something caught his eye. He reached down, picked it up, and held it out so both of them could see it. It was a piece torn from a shipping tag; a partial Arabic character was printed on it.

The men exchanged a look; Bobby made a thumbs up gesture and they both smiled. The captain put the tag in the zipper pocket across the chest of his anorak. He had no idea what he had, only that he and Bobby had found it in a secret room in a barn in the middle of Ireland. With Bobby leading the way they crawled out the hole they had come through. With difficulty they pushed the bales back in place and carefully moved to the door. The captain opened it about two inches. The rain had stopped. He opened it a little further and they slipped out into the night. The captain leaned down and with great care began to relock the door. Suddenly a dog barked. Then it barked again. A light went on in the farm house. There was a shout. Then a shot.

They ran zig-zagging across the field, jumping over the electric fences or sometimes, charged with adrenaline, just knocking them down. They reached the hedgerow and threw themselves over it, rolling as they hit the ground. By this time a spotlight had come on and was sweeping the field they had just vacated, and they could hear automatic rifle fire. The crack and whizz of the bullets gave them the pattern, a skill every soldier learns in battle.

"Shoots left, he does."

"Yes, he does," the captain responded, and they moved to the right.

The Range Rover, with Mick at the wheel, came down the lane, pausing briefly to let Bobby and the captain climb aboard. One round put a hole through the SUV's side and safely exited through the hole it created in the window on the other side.

CHAPTER EIGHT

30 September — Washington, D.C. —

Tracy poured herself a cup of coffee in the common room of the Hill Center, when down the hall came an enormous African American man in his twenties who seemed to her as big as a bear dressed in a housepainter's white jumpsuit. In spite of his size there was a kind of good natured charisma about him. His name was stitched in red thread across his left breast, "Weldon Shelcraft."

He held out a tablet to Tracy, and she saw the target as well as Weldon's drawing. The target was a picture of a marina with sailboats. His simple drawing caught the essence: the boat shapes, the masts, almost as if he were standing out on the water looking into the harbor at the moored boats.

"Tracy, will you look at this! It's my best yet," he said handing it to her.

She looked at the tablet and then at Weldon. "Wow. No question that's a hit. I particularly like the boat outlines."

"Are we still on for Sunday?" Weldon asked. "I thought Sarah and her friend might like to walk a little of the Appalachian Trail. There's a fire tower..."

"Weldon, you know the answer." Tracy said. "Sarah told her whole class about the cave. Now they all want to go on any trip you're leading. Even the mommies are happy." Then, giving him another smile, "Could we take two more...?"

As Tracy and Weldon were standing there, an earthy woman in her fifties with thick red hair, sitting in a very sophisticated—almost sleek—electric wheel chair, rolled around the corner. Once she had been beautiful. She was no longer that, but something more interesting. Strong character with a rakish manner; you knew she'd had an interesting life. She was dressed in a subtle moss green kaftan. No restriction to bind her as she sat. It was very stylish; she had green suede slippers on her feet.

"Weldon, are you out proselytizing a new generation for Mother Earth?" she said with a heavy Louisiana accent.

Weldon was delighted and surprised to see her, and he leaned over and gathered her up in his arms.

"Michael told me you were coming back this week. How was China?" Then, remembering Tracy, he said, "Barbara, I'd like you to meet our newest viewer, Tracy Walsh. She's an anthropologist on the faculty. Tracy this is Barbara Strickland."

Tracy looked at the woman, and was visibly moved. Barbara Strickland was one of the most famous scientists in the world, like Margaret Mead or Madame Curie. She had been a model for Tracy when she was in graduate school. "Professor Strickland... it's an honor. I never ...."

"Thought a Nobel Laureate physicist would be a remote viewer. Neither did the physicist. Actually, though, my dear, there are rather a lot of us who think consciousness is the fundamental. Remote viewing is a way to experience the hypothesis. Einstein wrote a forward to Upton Sinclair's book on his nonlocal consciousness experiments with his wife, *Mental Radio*. Niehls Bohr. Wolfgang Pauli. Max Planck, Brian Josephson. Not everyone, of course... but more than you'd ever think. For another time perhaps." Stopping, she wheeled closer. "Could I have a cup from that pot you're holding?"

Tracy picked up a cup and saucer and poured the coffee.

"Milk... sugar?" she said, still processing Barbara Strickland being a viewer.

"Just black thank you. We do have good coffee here," Barbara said. "Michael buys it at that coffee place on M Street."

Weldon put his cup in the sink, rinsed it out and put it in the dishwasher. "I've got to go. . . glad you're back Barbara. You've got to give me another chance to get back at you..."

"Anytime you think you're ready Weldon. But don't get cocky..."

Barbara wheeled her chair over to where Tracy sat and said with a smile, "Grudge match backgammon. Let's sit over here, my dear, and you can tell me how Michael turned you into one of his guinea pigs."

"I volunteered," Tracy said.

"Me too," Barbara responded.

Tracy stood up and said to Barbara, "I can't tell you what an honor it is to get to know you. And you doing this, and believing in it, really helps me. I have to pick up my daughter Sarah. She goes to school right around the corner. But can we talk again?"

"I am glad to know you. Of course we can. We'll have some fun," Barbara said, and reached out to take Tracy's hand and squeeze it.

Half an hour later in front of the Immaculate Heart School, Tracy stood near Sarah who was talking with a classmate; they were deep in conversation. Her mother radar was on, but mostly she had tuned the children out the way mothers do: aware, watchful, but not listening. She was looking for someone, waiting for them to drive up.

"Penny said it was true, Sarah. Her father said they do something that takes you out of your body..."

Sarah listened to her friend, and in her most dismissive manner, responded, "That's just silly... you're a silly... Mommy..."

Before Tracy could answer, Michael, dressed in sweats, jogged up, saw Tracy and stopped. He was not whom Tracy had been expecting, but when she saw him her face lit up.

"Michael."

"Hi. What brings you here?"

"Sarah. This is where my daughter goes to school. That's her. Funny it being just around the block."

Sarah came over and looked up at the adults expectantly.

"Sarah, this is Professor Gillespie..."

"You're the man from the witch's house," Sarah said looking at Michael. Then she looked back at Jennifer, who was staring at them.

"Sarah, please..."

Michael just laughed. "Is that what you call it?"

As Sarah started to answer a car pulled up, a man in his thirties at the wheel. His window rolled down and he leaned out saying, "Sarah, hurry..."

Tracy, speaking softly, leaned towards Michael, "You get to meet the whole family." She then turned back and called out, "Keith... come here a minute. I want you to meet Michael Gillespie."

Keith's manner visibly cooled as he saw Tracy; however, he was trapped in good manners and started to get out. He was a man of medium height, conservative in dress and haircut, wearing black glasses. When he heard Michael's name he stopped and stood with the car door between himself and Michael and Tracy. Coolly he said, "Hello," then focused on Sarah, telling her, "Hurry up, the show starts in 20 minutes and the traffic is bad."

Sarah was already moving as her father was speaking, waving and saying, "Bye, Jennifer. Bye Mommy." She got almost to the car then stopped, turned, and ran back to hug her mother. She sensed the tension between her father and Michael, and only looked at him quickly. Then ran back, and got into the car, and Keith pulled off. Tracy and Michael were left standing on the sidewalk.

"Oh, Michael I'm sorry. It's..."

"I understand... Awkward. It's awkward. Don't worry. I know you've only been separated a few months. These things are tough," Michael said, reaching out and touching her arm. Both were aware of the contact.

Later that night Tracy and Sarah were sitting on Sarah's bed. Tracy was brushing her daughter's long hair with careful, gentle strokes. Sarah was in her nightgown.

"Mommy, are you becoming a witch?"

"Good heavens, Sarah, what would make you think such a thing?" Tracy replied, wounded that her daughter would think that.

"Jennifer and Penny are afraid of that place where you go. They say that witches live there. And Daddy said tonight that what you are doing is dangerous and silly. Is it dangerous? Will something bad happen to you?"

Tracy's stomach lurched as she heard her daughter's question. She felt exposed and sabotaged at the same time. For a moment she wasn't sure how to answer. How much was too much? How much was too little? She finally settled on the simple truth. "There is nothing about witches at Professor Gillespie's laboratory. I am exploring how the human mind works, because I need to know those things in my own research. We've talked about that. You know you will be with Daddy for six weeks this summer, when I go to Brazil. But as for what I am doing here, would you like to come and watch me do it?"

"But it's spooky."

"What's spooky about it?"

"I don't know, but Jennifer and Penny say you're being medium.... Why does size matter?... talking to ghosts..."

"Well this is one time when Jennifer and Penny don't know what they're talking about. I've never met a ghost, and wouldn't know what to say if I met one."

"I would just scream."

"You might scare him away."

"Good. . . oh, I love you, Mommy."

"I love you too, sweetheart. Now get into bed and let's say prayers."

Sarah scooted down; Tracy tucked the covers up to her chin and for a moment they just looked into each other's eyes. Then they both closed their eyes and began, "Our Father who art in heaven. Hallowed be thy name..."

After Sarah was asleep Tracy went into her living room and sat looking into the gas fire. The evening with Sarah had left her shaken. As she sat there thinking about it, the door bell rang. She got up to answer it, looked through the peephole and frowned, then opened the door to Keith.

"Sorry, I didn't call first, Tracy. But I had a late meeting and needed to come ho... to your apartment. I have to get the canceled checks out of the hall closet. It's coming up to the end of the year, and we need to decide how we're going to file taxes."

"Of course. Would you like something to drink? A cup of coffee?"

"Coffee's fine."

Tracy went into the kitchen to pour the coffee, leaned for a moment against the wall, and took a deep breath. When she came back Keith was going through a cardboard banker's box filled with papers.

"Can I ask you something?" she said.

"What is it?" he answered without looking at her.

"Did you tell Sarah that the research I was doing at the Hill Center was dangerous and silly?"

"Hill Center? Research? You make it sound like it's in the real world. What you mean is that psychic New Age crap, where you're talking with spirits or whatever. With your background, Tracy, you'd think you'd know better."

"Keith, your rigid physicalism coupled with your rigid religiosity, which is a complete contradiction if you could just see it, are two of the reasons we're not together anymore. Altered states of consciousness are mainstream anthropology. I'm sorry to tell you that but it's true. Remote viewing has nothing to do with..."

". . . Tracy, anybody with half a brain knows that astrology, remote viewing, channeling, whatever you call it..."

"Astrology, remote viewing, and channeling are three different subjects. I don't care whether you understand that or not. What I do care about is that you not tell our daughter something that scares and worries her. She's got enough to..."

"Okay . . .Okay, you're right. That was off base. But..." Keith stopped in mid-word and they both turned and saw

Sarah, holding Miss Pibbs, her favorite doll, standing in the doorway.

CHAPTER NINE

7 October — Cartegena, Columbia —

The lights along the wharves in the dock area of the city left pools of light like steps in the darkness, except where a ship was being worked; there, in contrast, it was as bright as day. Enormous world-traveling ocean container ships were spaced along the concrete wharves. Towering over them were huge cranes. On their decks were 40-foot-long steel shipping containers piled eight high. Further down the docks, there were moorings for smaller ships like bulk cargo freighters. One of these was the blue hulled *Wang May*. It was dark and there was nothing going on around her. The only person visible was the watch amidships; the rest of the crew was in the city on shore leave.

A black van drove down the wharf and stopped across from the freighter's gangway. Two men got out, opened the van doors and brought out a sturdy aluminum case. Carrying it between them, they walked up the gangway, speaking Spanish as they did so. One was considerably older than the other, who looked to be in his twenties.

The watch officer, alerted by the seaman on watch, stood at the head of the gangway to meet them. He was Korean, and there was a tenseness to his reception.

"Have we ever met?" he challenged.

"At the soccer match, don't you remember," the older man responded. That was the introduction code, and all three relaxed.

"Where are you coming from?"

"We drove down from Panama City. Started two days ago when we got notice you were coming in to Cartegena."

"Do you know what's in the case?"

"No? Do you?"

"No, we're just doing what we were told. Deliver it to you."

"Us too, so let's do it."

The watch officer took them into the ship and down a corridor to stairs. They went down several decks, then along a corridor and through a steel bulkhead door into an enormous storage deck filled with containers of all kinds, including a sailboat on a cradle with its mast shipped. They came to a room within the cavernous room.

"Smaller things are stored here," the officer said as he unlocked the rolling door and raised it. Guided by the officer, the two men put the case on a shelf and secured it with cables. When they were finished the officer handed them an envelope, and they all turned to backtrack the way they had come, the officer leading the way.

After he was far enough ahead to be out of earshot, the younger man said, "It was smaller than I thought."

"They did something to it," the older man answered. "Simplified it I was told. It seems0 size is important."

At the gangway head they all shook hands, and the two men walked down, got into their van, and drove away.

CHAPTER TEN

11 October — Washington, D.C. —

Tracy hurried across the Georgetown University campus into the medical center. She walked down the hallway until she came to a door marked "Maureen Goldman, M.D., Psychiatry." She sat down in the waiting room and looked at her watch; she was just on time. A minute later the inner door opened and a well-dressed stout woman in her late forties stood in the doorway.

"Come in, Tracy," she said, and turned and went back into her counseling room, Tracy following her. They both sat down and just looked at each other for a moment. The physician was a powerful but detached motherly presence. When she spoke they fell into their pattern for these sessions.

"How are things going?"

"It's been tough, Goldie. Keith and his judgments… he never lets up."

"And how does that make you feel?"

"Like it always has. Judged. Found wanting. Below that, angry. What makes me really angry is that he's running me down to Sarah."

The doctor showed no emotion but her tone was supportive when she said, "What is he saying?"

"Recently most of it centers on the research I'm doing with Michael Gillespie. Keith knows I'm vulnerable to what Sarah says, so he attacks me through her."

"What did he say?"

"What he's told Sarah is that he's worried that this research could be dangerous... of course that's ridiculous and I know he knows that. But it's a chance for him to make me seem weird. Goldie, this work is fascinating... I'm looking into my mind and being open to something I didn't even know was there. I've been doing work with primitive tribes, intuition, and trance states for years. I know now I did not understand them correctly. Now I'm getting to experience the shamanic path and test it for myself in the middle of Washington D.C.."

"Why do you think this is so alarming Keith?"

"Once... we'd been married only about two years... he went down to Haiti with me. I wanted to study the role of indigenous healers there. Keith just wanted a break so he usually just sunbathed, played golf, or lay on the hotel bed reading. One evening, though, he went with me to a ceremony. The healer was a woman, and in her trance, she danced on broken bottles and bit off the head of a live chicken... It was gross, but amazing."

"How did Keith react?"

"It wasn't until we got back to the hotel and I started making notes that he kind of went crazy. He said I was satanic and sick for even being interested in something like that. He apologized later, but now he's comparing my remote viewing with that trip to Haiti. He's telling Sarah what I'm doing is sick and dangerous."

"Tracy, Keith is threatened. He's an engineer, a conservative field. He's a conservative man, a kind of fundamentalist Catholic who, you told me, was very conflicted even about using birth control. You picked this man because his conservatism seemed a compensation for things a part of you saw as far-out... things you were doing in anthropology. Choosing Keith as your partner was a way of anchoring yourself in the safe world you knew as a child. A safe haven if things got too weird. Your pain is partly tied up with having to give up the past... the safe haven... the safe haven is no longer safe. There is also the issue of your success. Keith holds traditional values about men and women. For ten years, you were exciting because you skirted the edge but didn't go over."

"Now, by becoming an active participant instead of remaining an observer... I've gone over."

"For Keith, yes. But complicating it, imagine how he feels seeing you get enormous feedback, almost all of it positive... the Richardson for instance. It puts Keith in an emotionally impossible position. You act weird and win; he acts appropriate to his values and goes nowhere."

"What can I do?"

"You're doing fine. Just keep doing what you are doing, with one exception."

"Thanks, Goldie... but what's the exception?"

"Keith is right about your being involved in the Hill Center's experiments. His reasons are wrong, but the recommendation is right. Tracy, reaching down into your unconscious to extract images is a dangerous activity at this moment. You could stimulate long repressed feelings that you are not prepared to cope with."

"Goldie. I'm a scientist. I have to go where my research leads. If I don't do that...who am I? Besides, my research is the only part of my life that's working."

"Tracy. I can only tell you what I believe to be in your best interest."

CHAPTER ELEVEN

16 October — Langley, Virginia —

A black government car drove up the George Washington Expressway, the Potomac River on its right as it moved through the trees and past old Civil War gun emplacements with their carefully preserved cannon. Leonard Belmore rode in the back reading a tablet and a briefing book, prepping for what was coming. The car wended its way out past McLean, Virginia, to the front gates of the CIA at Langley, where it paused for a moment to let the guard check Belmore's ID against a list. The car stopped at the entrance, and he got out and entered the building, where he showed his government ID a second time. He crossed the entrance foyer, its marble wall incised with stars to commemorate the agency's fallen heroes.

Belmore asked directions from the guard, took the elevator and got off at the executive floor; the walls were paneled in polished brown wood, and oil paintings and antiques decorated the space. He turned and walked down the hall until he saw a small sign reading, "Deputy Director — Operations." In the outer office a trim official-looking Black woman sat behind a wooden desk with a sign reading, "Denise Mailman."

"Good morning, Mr. Belmore," she said when she saw him come in. "The Deputy Director will be with you in a moment. Can I get you some coffee or tea?"

"Coffee'll be fine, black. Thank you," he answered, and went over to sit on the couch.

The woman pushed an intercom buzzer and said into it, "Manuel, could we have a cup of black coffee please? Thank you."

A moment later a Philippine steward entered from a side door with coffee on a silver tray. As Belmore began to drink it, the door opened and a large bulky man came out. Caught with his cup and saucer in his right hand, Belmore was momentarily off-balance. He put the cup down and stood up.

"Leave it. We'll get you another one. Come in. I'm Sam Kassimir, the Deputy Director," he said, putting out his hand. He was a big beefy man, bald, and his Turkish genes had given him a very heavy beard. They shook hands and Belmore followed Kassimir into his inner office. Seated around the conference table in the Deputy Director's office were the Director himself, a political appointee in his early forties who Belmore had met once in Warrenton, Virginia, at an Airlie House conference when he held another post, and two other men, neither of whom he knew.

"Director, gentlemen," Kassimir said as Belmore stood next to him. "This is Leonard Belmore. He's up from Miami on the redeye. He has some information on our situation. The Director and I felt the Ops team should hear it personally, if you agree, Director."

The Director, who was four months into his appointment and out of his depth, nodded his head. "Of course, Sam. Let's hear what he has to say."

Taking out his tablet, Belmore looked around the table and began. "We've got some people inside Columbia, one based in Cartegena. Independent of DEA. NSC put the initial group together in the 80s for the Contras and has kept them running on a low key basis ever since. One of them reported yesterday that Roberto Carnava, an upper-level logistical type in the cartel, got really drunk or stoned the other night and said the U.S. was in for a hell of a surprise. He told our informant that a group you can hardly believe could stay in the same room have gotten together in a common project they all want. He said they come from the Japan Freedom Battalion, the Italian Red Brigade, what's left of the IRA and various ISIL Muslim groups as well as government operatives from North Korea. Also some really extreme White supremacy militia types in the U.S.. According to our informant, Carnava said they had gotten hold of a bomb that would make the World Trade Center look like a fire cracker."

Belmore put down his tablet and looked around the room. "Does any of this make sense to you all?"

The man to Belmore's right asked, "How reliable is this source?"

Belmore looked to the Deputy Director for permission to reveal his source, and Kassimir nodded affirmatively. "He's... Carnava's driver. His information has proven to be very reliable. He's the brother-in-law of Carnava's wife's sister."

"Family," the first man responded.

"That's right."

Kassimir asked, "Did you get a time frame?"

"No, nothing specific. But the sense was soon. There apparently has been some sort of disagreement as to where this is going to go off, and that has affected the timing."

The second man, who had remained silent until then, asked, "Can we get anything more?"

"Honestly, I don't know. I've already communicated that request, but I don't think so. If I had to put a probability on it

I'd say twenty percent tops. In the morning Carnava didn't remember what he'd said, so the driver can't bring it up."

The first man asked, "What's the cartel involved for? They're not political in that sense."

The second man answered before Belmore could speak. "Because they know all the best paths into the U.S., right Belmore?"

Kassimir asked, "How many people have had access to this information?"

"Myself and my deputy. Until I talked with you, sir, I had nothing to suggest the material was real except past experience with this man."

"You did good, Belmore," Kassimir responded. "Your file says you're not married. I've ordered TDY orders cut to transfer you up here for a while. Any problems?"

"None I can't take care of, sir."

"Then let me introduce you to Stanley Potter," Kassimir said, indicating the first man. "And this is Herbert Waterman. They'll brief you on what's going on. I'll tell you this, though. A five kiloton nuclear device is somewhere in the international terrorist network, and it is on the move. There is some kind of operation underway that involves the rare cooperation of virtually every major terrorist organization in Europe, Asia, and the Middle East. We think it's being financed by the North Koreans, but we don't really know. It's being well-financed though. The information you got... well, it adds to what we already know. We're talking here about a bomb twice the size of the one that took out Hiroshima, and it seems to be headed somewhere here in the United States. This is not a happy picture."

"Yes sir. I understand."

"There is nothing... I mean nothing, more important than this crisis. We have to stop this or it could precipitate World War III."

CHAPTER TWELVE

7 November — Washington, D.C. —

Michael was in the midst of a seminar with his graduate students. Enlargements of specific experiments were displayed on the three large video screens behind him. Each showed the target photo as well as the viewers' drawings and their commentary, including the concept-by-concept evaluation as to its accuracy. Also a range of biometric data including the blood pressure, 32-point brain scans, and voice analysis of both the viewer and the monitor conducting the session. Tracy came into the lecture hall after he had started and sat down in the back.

"The precognitive series we are running now is producing data averaging eighty-two percent accurate. Results like these, I suggest, carried out with such strict controls, force us to rethink what we believe about time, space, and consciousness," Michael said, then asked, "How many of you are running experiments this week?" Several hands went up. "O.K. I want you to pay particular attention to getting color imagery. We're going to try and see whether some colors are easier to perceive than others." The bell rang, and Michael ended the class. "That's it. Talk to Karen about scheduling your sessions."

The students filed out, many of them acknowledging Tracy as they passed her; she was now clearly a part of the team. Finally the hall was empty except for Tracy, who had remained seated. Michael looked up as he collected his notes and put his tablet into a leather messenger bag, saying, "Our session's scheduled in a few minutes."

Tracy came down the steps to the lecture platform, and the two of them walked out of the building and down the street towards the Hill Center.

As they walked Michael asked, "How's it going?"

"Okay, I guess."

"It doesn't look Okay."

"Oh, Michael, so much in my life is great. But the part that isn't is really rotten."

"Is our work together. . ."

"No... Michael. You've been great. You're one of the good things that's happened. It's Keith... and doing the right thing about Sarah. God it's hard taking your life apart."

"Would it help if I talked with Keith and explained this research?"

"Keith doesn't really care. It's just a club to hit me with. If he did have an opinion it would be religious and you don't need that. Even my therapist is concerned that I'm mucking about with my unconscious."

They walked in silence for a moment, but when they got to the Hill Center and were standing in the brick courtyard before the steps, Michael said, "Maybe your therapist is right. Are you sure you want to continue?"

"Do you want me to?"

"What I want is unimportant, Tracy. You need to weigh it against what your therapist told you... and your evaluation as a scientist. This is something only you can decide. But yes, okay, I would miss you, a lot," Michael looked into her eyes as he spoke, and she saw in them what she felt herself, a growing love.

"I have thought about it quite a lot. Let's do the session," and she led the way to the egg.

Having settled into a routine it took just a few minutes to set things up. Tracy tilted her chair back to her favorite position and lay back against the cushions. Michael adjusted the lights so that the room was in twilight and logged in as Tracy closed her eyes and took a deep breath.

"You are here in the egg. It is now three o'clock in the afternoon the 7th of November. Go forward in time to three o'clock the 28th of November."

In Tracy's mind, with her closed eyes, there was darkness followed by brief watery flashes of unidentifiable images, dissolving to flashes of recent memories, which flickered and extinguished. Then, lower down in one corner, the image of the lab building, seen at an angle looking down, hovering at tree top level. The image zoomed in, then pulled back. It was in a watery focus. Then blackness. Tracy fidgeted, and became increasingly frustrated.

"Michael, I can't do it... I can't seem to hold my focus and get Keith, Sarah, and Goldie out of my head."

"Not a problem," Michael said soothingly. "Let's take a break. Session suspended, time code now," he said, pressing a button on his tablet. He brought the lights back up, and Tracy tilted her chair to a more upright position. She got up and paced, frustrated with herself.

"How about going up to my office and leaving this for the moment."

The two of them walked back to his office where the open French doors looked out onto the black iron balcony.

Michael tried to lighten things by just making casual conversation. "Look at this weather. These fall days are our reward for living through Washington summers. You know, because of the heat the British used to consider the city a hardship post."

Tracy smiled at Michael, recognizing what he was doing, and tried to respond in kind. "Well, with my life I'm beginning to agree with the British.... It was funny in there... I couldn't get an image..."

"No big deal . . . everybody gets blocked sometimes."

Tracy's eyes brightened as she went out onto the balcony.

"Oh, I've never been out here before Michael. . . look!" She pointed down past the walled garden to where a team of girls were playing field hockey in the schoolyard. Another cluster of younger girls were jumping rope, and Sarah was amongst them.

Michael looked out over the schoolyard to where Sarah was playing. "Is that Sarah down there?" he asked.

"Yes, aren't they cute? I remember being that age and doing exactly the same thing."

Tracy leaned back and stretched, now much more relaxed. Michael saw this. Tracy understood what he had in mind and smiled at him. "Michael, you're a real seducer."

"I do what I can," he answered with a smile. "Wait here," he said, going into his office and coming back with two biohoods with their trailing cables plugged into his tablet, and a tripod.

He put the tripod down and secured the tablet with its camera pointed at Tracy.

"Here, put this on," Michael said, handing her one of the cloth bio-helmets and putting on the other. "It's nowhere near as sophisticated as the egg, but it's still useful."

Tracy did as he asked. When she was settled, looking out across from the balcony he said, "This is a continuation of session 442," as he glanced down at a readout from the tablet. "Viewer is Tracy Walsh, interviewer Michael Gillespie. Time and date code now," he said, pressing the tablet again. "Go forward in time. It is three o'clock in the afternoon on the 28th of November."

Tracy closed her eyes. In her mind an image began to emerge. Sarah was playing with the other children. "I can see the children much as they are now. I can see Sarah. They're playing hopscotch. I can hear their squeals and screams." She paused for a moment, then continued, "There is the flickering quality like a mirage as a second image overlays this one: the children continue to play but suddenly the trees blow over and the brick wall of the school explodes. Bricks fly past as the chain link fence bulges and blows away. The children burst into flames and disappear."

Tracy's face crumpled in horror and she screamed, "Noooooooo!"

Michael quickly moved to her side to enfold her in his arms.

"Tracy. . . Tracy. . . it's all right. Tracy. . . it's all right."

She pulled back and continued screaming, "Nooo . . . nooo . . . . no. . ."

The children, their game interrupted by her scream, looked up at the balcony, shading their eyes against the sun with their hands.

Tracy fainted as Michael reached for her, and she fell to the balcony floor banging her head on the iron railing as she went down.

She woke up lying on the couch in Michael's office. He was kneeling over her and holding some smelling salts from the first aid kit lying open next to him. His other hand was behind her head pressing a gauze pad to her scalp, which was bleeding badly.

"Michael... It was horrible. They lit up like candles... they were consumed. I've never seen..." Tracy began sobbing into his shoulder as he leaned to embrace her. She was completely undone.

"Tracy, listen. We have to get you to the hospital. You're going to need stitches."

Tracy was silently shaking with her arms tucked in to Michael's embrace. Michael helped her up and called down the stairs for someone to bring a car around. He got Tracy down the stairs and into a car driven by one of the graduate students.

"We need to get her to the ER."

"No problem. Get in."

Michael climbed in the back still holding Tracy, and they drove the few blocks to the Georgetown Hospital emergency room. The driver pulled the car in under the portico, jumped out and grabbed a wheelchair, where several were lined up.

With Michael's help they got Tracy into the chair. Michael was still putting pressure on the dressing on Tracy's head, but blood was beginning to seep out, a little rivulet running down her neck.

"What's the problem? How can I help?" A nurse was suddenly there. She took in what was going on, assessed it, and directed Michael to an ER bed. An orderly came, and they got her into the gurney and raised the back until she was almost sitting. Tracy was distracted, out of it, and neither cooperated nor resisted.

The nurse took Michael's dressing off and looked at the wound.

"She's going to need stitches. I am afraid you are going to have to leave, sir. Alan, will you ask Dr. Henderson to come to seven?" The orderly left, returning in a minute with a young resident who examined the wound and directed a head x-ray be taken, the wound be cleaned again, and Tracy prepared for sutures. The doctor went off to another patient and the orderly stepped out with him. The nurse helped Tracy undress and put on a gown. She cleaned out the wound and got out the necessary surgical pack. As she was setting it up the orderly came in and helped Tracy into a wheelchair. He looked at the nurse, she nodded, and he pushed her to X-ray where they took the images. Then he pushed her back to the ER bed.

The doctor came back a few minutes later with the X-ray film, looked at it, and told Tracy, "There's no concussion and no fracture. Head wounds bleed a lot, and you've got quite a gash." With that the ER team fell quickly into a practiced rhythm. They had done it countless times, and said hardly a word. They anesthetized her scalp, leaving it numb. Tracy just lay there, with the images from her vision coming and going in her mind.

When the procedure was finished and they were cleaning up, the young doctor asked, "What happened?"

"I'm not sure," Tracy responded. "It was horrible...," Tracy's face began to crumple, and tears run down her cheeks.

"I don't understand, what were you doing?"

"I was doing a remote viewing experiment."

"What kind of experiment?"

Tracy began, "An experiment in altered states of consciousness. I'm Professor Tracy Walsh. I'm on the faculty here."

"Whatever it was, Professor, it has left you very shaken. I'm actually more concerned about your emotional state than your head wound. It says on your chart you're a patient of Dr. Goldman's. I'm going to call her and ask her to come over." He handed her a paper cup with a tablet and a glass of water. "Take this, it will help you relax."

A few minutes later Maureen Goldman came into the enclosure.

"Hi, Goldie. I'm fine. Really."

"Who's with you? Can they walk you over to my office?"

"Yes, but I'm fine…"

Michael appeared through the drapes and looked at Tracy and Goldman.

"I heard that; I'll walk you over."

"Twenty minutes. I have to change something," Goldman said, and walked out.

With his arm around her shoulder, Michael walked with Tracy through a series of corridors to the other side of the building. They were some minutes early and went outside in what was now twilight to sit on a bench.

"God. At least this was Keith's day to pick up Sarah, and she stays overnight with him because tomorrow is Saturday. It is Saturday tomorrow, right?"

Michael looked at her and smiled. "Yes, tomorrow is Saturday."

"Thank God for small favors," Tracy said with meaning.

"This drug is making me dopy. Oh, Michael, thank you. Thanks for being there," Tracy said, and kissed Michael on the lips, and he responded. When they separated Michael said, "We have to go; we have two minutes to get to Goldman. Do you want to go alone, or do you want me to go with you?"

"I'll be fine. Call me later," Tracy said, and went back into the building. By the time she got to Goldman's door she was fidgety and defiant, knowing she was about to be admonished. She went in and sat down. Goldman came from around her desk and sat in her chair and the ritual began. "You apparently suffered an hallucination that caused a temporary break with reality. Are you comfortable telling me as much as you remember about what happened?

"I was doing a remote viewing session. I couldn't focus in the shielded room, so we took a break, and went out onto the balcony. To my surprise it looked down into the schoolyard of Sarah's school. We picked up the session there, and I was supposed to describe something that I would be shown on the 28th. But as I looked, oh, Goldie...the children burst into flames as the trees blew over and the brick wall of the school exploded." As Tracy spoke, her emotions, although drugged, were still intense and tears started to flow down her face.

"It was like a vision... I guess. It was completely real, yet like a hologram in front of my eyes. The buildings went. Then the chain link fence blew out... Bricks were flying towards me. It was like a bomb. The children burst into flame... like grease spots, or candles. Yet all this time I saw the children down below, Sarah playing hopscotch. I've never experienced anything like that double quality before, but I couldn't hear anything. It was like I was in a bubble... an observer. Oh God, Goldie it was so real."

"Let me propose an interpretation," Goldman said with real compassion. "The explosion is your unconscious mind's presentation of the psychological explosion going on in your life. This is what we've been talking about. You were relaxed out there. We've already talked about your attraction to Michael and your conflict about that. You are also concerned about the effect all of this is having on Sarah. You looked over and saw her, just as you entered an altered reality state. At that moment you hallucinated."

"What I saw was real, Goldie."

"Hallucinations appear to be real. That's why they're scary."

"It was real. It wasn't like an hallucination."

"Tell me about your life right now, Tracy."

"All right... I'm upset."

"Don't you see, your unconscious gave you a perfectly appropriate image, an explosion."

"Maybe you're right, Goldie. I don't know. Look... on the way over here, Michael suggested I should stop working in the experiments."

"I agree, and good for him."

"I'm sorry, Goldie but I don't agree. I want to know what this is about. I'm a scientist."

The two women looked at one another, and both understood they had arrived at a crossroads. What came next would determine their relationship from that point forward.

"I'm sorry, Goldie," Tracy said as she got up and left. When she got to the door, Goldman responded, "So am I."

Tracy went downstairs and found Michael waiting for her. He looked at her, said nothing, and just followed her as she went out the door and down the steps. Tracy started walking home with Michael, but then he said," I want to see something. Do you mind a little detour?"

"Not at all."

Michael continued past the lab and walked around the block to the school yard. The far wall was bathed in the harsh light of a security floodlight, with added pools created by the streetlights behind him on the other side of the sidewalk. He laced his fingers in the wire mesh and looked across the grass and blacktop.

"There's going to be a horrible explosion here, Michael. I've never had an experience like that."

"Something is going to happen, I agree. Let me not say anything until I have gone through the data. I'm going to walk you home now. I think you need to go to bed. I'm afraid you're going to have a terrible headache."

As they walked to her flat on the top two floors of what had once been a single family house, Tracy told Michael what had happened with her therapist. When they got to her door there was an awkward pause while they both silently decided whether they should kiss or not, and settled for a long hug and a double cheek kiss.

"We're going to find out what this is, Tracy. I promise," Michael said as Tracy closed the door.

CHAPTER THIRTEEN

8 November — Washington, D.C. —

The next day, Michael cancelled his schedule for the morning and sat playing and replaying the digital record of Tracy's session: the audio, the visual, all the biometric data. Everything they had collected. Research had taught him that changes in brain function involving the cingulate could reveal which comments, which concepts, were most likely to be accurate. With each pass he searched for something, some previously unnoticed nuance that would give him insight. During the first part of the session, conducted in the egg where they got full data, there was nothing unusual about the session. Even if Tracy hadn't verbalized it, her biometric data would have shown her frustration about being unable to focus. She had a signature when she held intentioned focus.

Once they had gone out on the balcony he had less to go on. He had done the session mostly to help Tracy show herself she could do it. Neither of them began with any idea of what was about to happen. As he ran the data a pattern began to emerge. The audio track analysis showed several points where her voice was more emphatic. The bio-data showed the same timing, and all of it suggested Tracy was beginning a good high accuracy session. Then it all went haywire. One minute Tracy was fine, the next she was in crisis, wailing, and then she fainted. There was no lead-in, so what triggered this, he thought?

It was only on this third pass through the video that he noticed Sarah at the very edge of the image and realized that just as he had given Tracy the task statement she had looked down and must have seen her daughter. Tracy's feelings about her daughter, the sense impressions, the numinosity of seeing the child just as the directive for the task was given, had been the trigger; he was sure of it. But it was noon before he felt he really understood what had happened.

He leaned over and pushed the intercom button.

"Karen, is Gilbert in the house or has he already left for Vancouver?"

"He was down in his lab; I haven't seen him go out."

"Could you ask him to come up here?" Michael sat looking at his tablet reflectively in silence until Gilbert Exposito, a post-doc in electronic neuroscience, knocked on the jam of his open door.

"Come in Gilbert. Thanks for coming up."

Gilbert was a Costa Rican in his late twenties, at the university on a visiting fellowship. He was not fat but plump, and wore glasses with dark green frames. He looked like a particularly benign Buddha with different colored cable leads draped around his neck. As he came into the room he pushed his glasses back up on his nose.

"Yo. Great Leader?"

"When are you leaving?"

"Day after tomorrow, four in the afternoon, why? Have you seen the conference schedule? I have to present the brain entraining paper, first panel the next morning."

"Do you have time to look at something? I would really appreciate your thinking," Michael asked.

Gilbert picked up on Michael's intensity and asked, "What's going on?"

"Sit down," Michael said. Gilbert sat down and looked at him with his usual calm. Michael told him what had happened and what he had done, showing him the record as he talked.

"Up to 4 minutes 18, she looks on track to be correct," Gilbert said. "Then she goes into crisis. So what's your hypothesis?"

"Her psychiatrist is Maureen Goldman; I think you know her," Michael said, and Gilbert affirmed it with a nod. "It's her view that Tracy had a breakdown because I induced her into an altered state. She saw her child and all the explosions going on in the divorce and its effect on Sarah caused a kind of breakdown."

"Yes, I see your point," Gilbert replied.

"It makes me very uncomfortable that I may have caused it."

"How could you have known Michael? You're not the viewer, you're the scientist. And that doesn't mean what drove that breakdown was not also an accurate remote viewing," Gilbert said, leaning forward. "You get that as well, right?" he said with some urgency.

"Yes, I've come to the same conclusion. I didn't tell you that because I wanted you to look at it cold. I wanted to see if you agreed," Michael responded.

"So what do we do?"

"I'm not sure," Michael answered.

"You think this explosion thing is real, don't you?"

"I think something is going to happen, Glibert. I just wish I knew what it was."

"Do you want me to cancel and stay here?"

"That would be lovely, but no. That paper needs to get on record and get submitted to a journal as soon as possible.

The NIH is accepting research proposals, and I want you to be able to stay on focus, just as we discussed," Michael said, then added, "What I would like you to do is be the parallel monitor, and do every other session with me. But we won't discuss anything until we are finished."

Gilbert nodded his head in agreement. "We can start tomorrow if Karen can get everyone booked," he said standing up. "I will get my lab closed up in the next couple of hours. So let me know," he said as he left.

Later that evening, with Sarah at Keith's, Tracy walked over to Michael's house just a few blocks away. Even though they only lived a short distance apart in Georgetown, it was her first time going there, and she was surprised when she got to the address. She had walked by it many times not knowing who lived there. It was a small white wooden house with green shutters. Unlike the other houses it was set back from the sidewalk; very different from the mostly brick or stone row houses around it. It had a second floor over only the back half of the house, and every time she saw it she was amazed the little house had survived.

A white arbor covered with rose bushes over a white wooden gate opened into the front garden. Being smaller than the houses on either side, but on the same sized lot, also gave the house space for a little side yard and a brick terrace which was given privacy from the street by a white trellis across the street-side end. Rose bushes and other plants lined the garden, and an old brick herringbone walk led to the front door.

As she started up the walk the door opened, and Michael came out with a watering can to water the plants in urns on either side of the door. He looked up, saw her, and set the can down.

"Tracy, please… come in."

She entered a small foyer with a black and white tile floor. On the left side of the hall was the living room, into which he led her. It was furnished in a combination of good antique Shaker and Japanese furniture, with a comfortable couch and two chairs. A small fire burned in the grate. Miles Davis' *Sketches of Spain* was coming over the sound system.

Tracy sat on the couch facing the fire, and Michael joined her at the other end.

"Michael, I'll only stay a minute. I just had to come over and tell you that I have given this very deep consideration, and I am clear that what happened had nothing to do with any stress in my life, and it was not your fault. And you have no right to cut me off as if I were a child who was being inconvenient."

"I haven't cut you off. I just said I want you to think about stopping for a while."

"Tell me what my accuracy rate has been..."

"You're very good at remote viewing, Tracy. Of the concepts we can evaluate you probably average seventy five to eighty five per cent accuracy in your sessions ..."

"Then you'll admit that what I saw may be accurate?"

"Yes, I will admit that," Michael responded immediately, but then added, "It's something I take very seriously, but it's not the issue..."

"Yes, that is the issue. I think this is an accurate perception, Michael, and I want you to carry out the same experiment with the others... using the same time parameters."

They sat for a moment staring at each other, then Michael smiled at her.

"I came to the same conclusion after spending half the day analyzing your session and then talking to Gilbert, who analyzed the data himself and agreed. In return, though, I want your agreement that if no one else reports an explosion you will willingly refrain from participating in experiments for a while."

"And, if they do... and you get similar reports, I want your commitment that we'll see this through. I am very serious about this, Michael."

"You have it; I agree with you." Michael got up from the couch and paced.

"I have something else I need to surface, Tracy."

"What?"

Michael went back and sat down on the sofa.

"This is something I never thought I'd do. Tracy, I am attracted to you. It's unprofessional. I know it. But there it is."

Tracy's body relaxed and she smiled with both her mouth and her eyes. "I've been trying to figure out how to bring that up," she said with a laugh, then was serious again. "I have accepted that Keith and I are not going to get back together. I'm not in love with him. I'm not even sure I ever was, and he is not in love with me. It's like a part of me has come alive again," she said, looking into Michael's eyes. "You're the first man... I've really looked at in years... Oh that sounds so dumb... I don't have a lot of practice. It's funny."

Michael drew Tracy to him. "Well, let's start with something simple," he said, and kissed her. She responded and they both gave themselves over to their attraction for each other.

When they separated, Tracy said, "I'm so glad to get that out of the way," and they kissed again.

"Is it possible you could stay... I know Sarah..."

"Sarah is with Keith and won't come back until 3 p.m. tomorrow. Keith is taking her to Cirque du Soleil. That's why I was able to come over."

Michael took her hand and led her down the hall to his bedroom across the back of the house. They went in, slowly undressed each other, and climbed into Michael's king-sized bed with a goose down duvet. Tracy and Michael made love slowly. The music changed to Café Del Mar and then Bliss' *Living in Exile*. When it was over they both fell asleep, still touching.

In the morning Michael woke first. As he came out of the bathroom after showering, Tracy woke and held the sheet across her breasts as she pulled herself up in bed. Michael, with a towel wrapped around his waist, looked down on her.

"Oh God, Tracy. This is not something I expected... was looking for. You're not someone I can take lightly. I could fall in love with you. I think I have fallen in love with you. Because of that I have to take what Dr. Goldman said seriously."

"So do I, Michael. But I also have to acknowledge what I think is right. About us, and about my vision. I know I'm not as experienced in some things... but in my field... I trust my judgment more than Goldie's, or even yours. My vision could be wrong. I accept that. I do not accept that it was an hysterical hallucination."

Michael gave Tracy a new toothbrush, then went up the hall to the kitchen and finished fixing toast and scrambled mozzarella eggs, with chives from the garden, as she came in to join him. They sat and ate in the little breakfast nook with its bay window, and got used to each other.

When they were finished, Michael walked Tracy home and then walked to the lab. As soon as he was in his office, Karen came in.

"Constance Walters is scheduled as you asked," she said. "She'll be here in about 15 minutes, and I know she will want to go into the meditation room and connect. So, half an hour."

"Thanks, Karen"

"Should I open a file?"

"Yes," Michael said.

"What do I call it?"

Michael thought for a moment. "The Vision Probe."

Thirty minutes later a middle aged Black woman stood in the doorway to Michael's office, and he got up and gave her a hug.

"Constance, how are you doing? How's Herbert? Come in, sit down."

When they were settled and he had given her coffee, Michael asked her, "How are your art kids?"

"Oh, Michael, I have the most interesting group this year. Ten years old, deaf."

"Is art helpful with deaf kids? I mean I know art is important, but…"

"Blindness cuts you off from objects. Deafness cuts you off from ideas," Constance said, putting her cup aside. "Art helps them go through the door of ideas."

A few minutes later they walked down to the egg and entered. "What are we doing, Michael?"

"Let me get set up," Michael responded, as they both settled into their routine.

"This is session 443," Michael said, glancing down at his tablet. "Viewer is Constance Walters. Interviewer Michael Gillespie. Time and date code now," he said, pressing the tablet again. "Take your three deep breaths. By the end of the third breath, your mind will be clear. Please go forward in time to 3 p.m. the 28th of November. You are life-sized and you are standing on the balcony of my office looking out. What are the impressions that come to you?"

For a moment Constance said nothing, just sat with her eyes closed. Then she opened them and looked at Michael. "There is some kind of flash. I sense a lot of heat. Incredible violence. Oh, my God, Michael, something very violent is happening."

Gilbert did the next session with John Sacks, a gay man who was a very successful interior designer based in old Chevy Chase. By having more than one person do the interviews they could at least diminish researcher expectation or the possibility of cueing. Gilbert did not know what Michael was hearing, nor did Michael know what was happening in Gilbert's sessions. All that came later.

Two hours later, Michael was in the egg once again, this time with Istaqa Chester, a Native American known as Coyote because his name meant Coyote Man in the language of the Hopis, his tribal group. He was a 28-year-old D.J. in the most popular club on M Street; a tightly muscled man with high cheek bones and deep red skin. Michael thought he looked frankly dangerous, like something out of the movies; a look he suspected Coyote cultivated. They had met when Coyote had knocked on Michael's door one day a year earlier to talk to someone about the precognitive dreams he had had since he was a child. They had hit it off immediately, talked most of that morning, and Coyote had walked away from their meeting thinking of Michael as a White shaman.

Just as Michael finished giving Coyote the task intention, he responded. "Incredibly loud sound... pressure... feels like the air itself is on fire... screams. An explosion, something big flying through the air. Let me draw that. All of the energy is moving in one direction like a great wind..."

As Michael broke for lunch, Gilbert and Jefferson Yu were going into the egg. He was glad to get outside as he walked down to a café on Wisconsin, his head filled with what he had heard, trying to make sense of it.

When he returned, Weldon Shelcraft was already waiting, ready for his session. They went down to the egg and as soon as the session began Michael began to hear the same kinds of impressions he had heard that morning

"Michael it's like a bomb went off..." were Weldon's first words.

At the end of the day, after he and Gilbert had each done another session, Michael sat in his office going over the data, looking at the various drawings the viewers had made, studying the consensual images that the sessions shared, as well as the sense impressions the various individuals had experienced in common.

By the time he closed up for the night he was sure that Tracy's original vision was as she claimed, not an hysterical reaction to stresses in her life, but a real event that lay less than three weeks into the future. As he walked home he wrestled with the obvious question: What could they do about it? It was an easy question, but it didn't have a easy answer. Go to the police? Right, he thought. "Yes, officer, my remote viewers are using nonlocal consciousness to see the future and they report a massive explosion will take place three weeks from now at 3 p.m. on the 28th of November." He could imagine

the reaction such a statement would provoke. He'd be lucky
to get out of the police station without a lawyer.

CHAPTER FOURTEEN

9 November — Greater Metropolitan Washington

The viewers were no less disturbed than Michael. Jefferson Yu, a slender middle-aged second generation Chinese man, had been one of Michael's viewers for about year. He had seen a television program in which Michael and the Center were featured, and that led him to go hear Michael speak. Afterwards he had gone up to Michael to talk about the hunches he had that had made him a success. That led to an invitation to come to the Center and his becoming a viewer. He loved the sessions in the egg, describing targets, and he was good at it.

But this was not targets, this was something else altogether. Yu owned a hardware store in Bethesda Maryland. His parents had come to the United States during the Maoist Cultural Revolution that killed forty-five million people, and their stories had shaped his mind. Social upheaval and terrorism made him very anxious. And he had been anxious ever since his remote viewing session.

When he had returned home from the session, his wife Zhi Ruo could see immediately something was wrong.

"Husband, what is it?"

"Lao po. Today I experienced something I cannot get out of my mind. Gilbert asked me to do a viewing for a target on the 28ᵗʰ. I saw a huge explosion. Of course I could not ask either Michael or Gilbert anything about it, but I could tell that Gilbert was very disturbed by what I said."

"What does it mean?"

"I don't know, but I am going to break protocol and ask Michael."

Istaqa Chester lived in a second floor apartment on M Street not far from the club where he worked. Although very popular, he was, in fact, a loner. So far as he knew there was only one other Hopi in D.C., and he lived in Reston, Virginia. They didn't really know each other because they came from different mesas, the strange massifs spread out across the Arizona desert above Flagstaff. On top there were ancient villages, with more houses down on the lands around the huge rock formations. Coyote came from Old Oraibi where he had lived until he went into the service. The other man came from Walpi. So they really only saw each other when they went back for tribal gatherings, like the Kachina dances, and maybe once or twice a year in Washington.

It was a strange life. At night he was "on" and crowds formed around him, as he did his sets, and sometimes he went out with groups. Women made themselves available, but he was always an outsider, at least in his own mind. Most of the time he was solitary. When he thought about it he felt that Michael and the other viewers, particularly Weldon, with whom he shared a passion for rock climbing, were his closest friends in what he thought of as the White world.

He had come back from his last viewing session, had an early dinner, and walked down to the C&O canal where he turned right and was soon in the woods. He didn't know what to make of what he had seen, except that it was something that was really going to happen. He wasn't going to wait for the 28th; he was going to ask Michael for a meeting and suggest that all the viewers attend. Even though the protocol was never to talk about sessions until they had been judged, he felt this could not wait.

After her session Constance Walters drove back to Capitol Hill where she and her husband, Herbert, had a brick rowhouse. Herbert was a captain in the Capitol Police. Their son was in the Air Force and their daughter was a marine biologist, both long out of the house. Twenty-eight years of marriage and still in love, Constance thought as she finished preparing dinner. As they sat eating in their kitchen she told him what she had experienced at the Hill Center. Herbert wanted to immediately report it.

"You can't, Herbert. I don't know what anyone else saw. I just know what I experienced, and it may not be accurate, or only a piece of it could be accurate. You know how it works."

"I know that if my wife thinks there is going to be an explosion that I take that seriously. You know I thought this remote viewing stuff was crazy, but after that briefing Michael did for all the spouses and partners, showing us all that stuff you all had done? Well, I changed my mind."

"Michael is analyzing all the data from the sessions he and Gilbert did. I am sure he is going to tell us what they conclude."

"Baby, I think I should still talk to the commander on this."

"And what would you tell him, dearest? Your wife is a psychic who thinks there will be an explosion. It would make you look foolish, and they might go to my school and ask questions. Nothing good will come of that," Constance said, clearing the table.

"Well then, what do you think we should do?" Herbert asked, helping put the dishes into the dishwasher.

"I think we should wait to see what Michael has to say, then decide," Constance replied, but then her expression changed. "But oh, God, what if it's true Herbert? What about my children? Is this some local thing up in Georgetown, a gas main or something, or could it affect us here on the Hill? I mean, what do people like us do? What should we believe?"

Herbert gathered his wife into his arms. "Let's give it a few days, and see what Michael and Gilbert come up with. And that Nobel Laureate physicist lady. I am sure she will have something to say about this."

"I'm sure she will too," Constance responded with her face pressed against Herbert's chest."

"Come on, enough's enough. Let's go to bed. We both have to be up at six-thirty," Herbert said, turning out the light, putting his arm around Constance and guiding her out of the kitchen.

CHAPTER FIFTEEN

**9 November — The American Side of the Gulf Stream
—**

The waters on the American side of the Gulf Stream were
mercifully calm after a hard crossing with 8-foot waves and
contrary winds. But it had been exhilarating, and the Korean
couple sailing the 37-foot Columbia were excited by what they
had just experienced. More than once it had verged on scary,
and they were happy to be out of the Stream. The boat and
the couple were a picture of millennial bliss. As they completed
a tack, a lobster boat piled high with traps and festooned with
large round buoys painted international orange pulled along
side. As it did so, ten or twelve of the large buoys seemed to
break loose and fall as a clump into the water. The young
Korean man at the helm quickly put his sail in irons and broke
out his boat hook. He reached over and snared one of the buoy
lines and began hauling up the clump of buoys.

Just as he got them alongside, a wickedly low slung 39-
foot Midnight Express powerboat came toward the sailboat.
Along its gray hull were the words U.S. Customs and Border
Protection, along with the agency's symbol and a wide slanted
blue line parallel to a narrow red one. It came racing towards
them powered by four 300 horsepower Mercury outboards; it
looked sleek and lethal, and was. As it drew near, a U.S. Coast

Guard helicopter came out of the sun and hovered above the sailboat and the lobster boat.

From the helicopter's speaker and on channel nineteen of the marine radio: "Lobster boat Vickie and sailboat Carpe Diem heave to and prepared to be boarded."

The Midnight Express herded the lobster boat over to the sailboat until the two craft were within fifteen feet of one another gently tossing in the sea. The Midnight Express then turned sharply and pulled alongside the lobster boat, and one of the customs agents jumped aboard. The three men on the lobster boat eyed him warily. A second agent stayed at the helm of the Midnight Express while a third manned a 50-calibre machine gun pointed at the boats. Hovering above the three boats was the helicopter with a crewmember pointing down another 50-calibre machine gun. It was tense and dangerous, and it was designed to be that way.

"May I see your papers, please?"

The lobster captain just groaned. "Oh...mon... this be the third time this week you board the Vickie. I be out of Bimini. Everybody know Sammy there. Whatchewwant? I just came over to pick up a new prop. Whatchyou think?

The agent was unmoved and his face was blank. "May I see your papers, please?"

The lobsterman went into the boat's cabin followed by the agent. Making a great show of it, he reached under the helm and pulled out a clear waterproof envelope containing papers for the boat and crew. The agent looked around the small cabin, picked up and put down several things, then turned and went back out to the stern deck, followed by Sammy. The agent looked over at his partners and shook his head negatively. He looked at the papers, spoke into the radio mic clipped to his orange vest, listened to his earpiece, and handed the papers back.

"Wait here."

The agent went back to the Midnight Express and it maneuvered around to the lee side of the sailboat. The whole process began again. There was barely room in the cockpit of the sailboat for the couple and the customs agent, because of the buoys the Korean man had pulled aboard rather than let them go, .

"May I see your papers?

"This is very strange. Do you have the right to..."

"Yes we do, sir. This will only take a minute. May I see your papers?"

The Korean woman said something to her partner in Korean, and went below, coming back with the boat's papers. The agent glanced at them, spoke into his mic, and listened to his earpiece for a moment...

"You are not American citizens. Is that correct?" The agent asked.

"No, Koreans... South Koreans."

"May I see your passports and visas please?"

Once again the young woman went below. This time she came back with two passports and visas that she handed to the agent.

"You don't own this boat?"

"No, we leased it. We're sailing from Miami up your East Coast. We came over from the Bahamas; we'd gone over to Nassau to see some friends," the man said, his manner open and courteous.

The agent handed back the papers, which the man in turn gave to the woman, who went back into the sailboat's interior.

"Will you come below with me, please, sir? Lead the way, please."

The man made a slight bow, turned, and led the agent below. Without a word the agent quickly and methodically went through the cabin, and forward into the fo'c's'le. Then he turned and came back to where they stood.

"Let's go topside, please. Would you lead the way?"

Once back on deck the agent looked across to his partners again, and shook his head. His partner pointed at the buoys. The agent reached down and picked one up. The rest were all strung together, making an awkward mass. The Korean couple and the lobstermen watched all this. The agent examined the buoy, seemed satisfied, motioned for his partner to come closer, then jumped back aboard the Midnight Express.

He looked back, and called, "You both may go."

"Yah.. mon, what about my buoys. Them things cost money," the lobster boat captain called.

The Korean man started to untangle the buoy lines in order to hand the buoys one at a time across to the lobster men who had pulled alongside. It was clumsy work and took time. Then he paused, seeming to think for a moment. The Customs agents were watching all of this but preparing to move off.

The Korean man called back, "Listen. Would you sell me one of your buoys? I'd like to keep it as a souvenir of this event. This whole thing has been like something out of a thriller movie."

"Yah...mon... you be keeping one. No charge. I be losing dem all without yah help."

The Korean man continued to pass the buoys over, until all but one had been returned; this buoy had been at the bottom of the pile and was significantly larger than the rest. While this was going on the customs boat and the Coast Guard helicopter moved off and were quickly gone.

CHAPTER SIXTEEN

13 November — Washington, D.C. —

Over the next several days Michael wrestled with what to do. If he was honest with himself, he did not see a clear way through.

For him it came down to one basic question: What do ordinary people do when they have reason to believe that a massive explosion is about to occur in their nation's capital city? It was such a simple question to state, as he had been doing in his head over and over; it was not so simple to answer. Going to the police, superficially the obvious move, seemed absurd and potentially humiliating.

He was considering sending an anonymous letter, yet was concerned with all the ways it could be tracked back to him: his fingerprints, the DNA in his saliva from sealing the envelope. All he knew about such things came out of movies, and he doubted any of it was accurate. It all went round and round in his mind unresolved. He particularly couldn't get the recurring image of himself facing a television camera out of his mind. It smacked of end of the world prophecies.

"How did you acquire this information about this explosion, Professor Gillespie?"

"From remote viewers participating in a program we are doing at my laboratory," he would start to say, but be interrupted. "Oh, you mean psychics, or is it fortune tellers?"

He envisioned a young brunette reporter asking the question with a taunting sneer as the camera was on him.

Part of the problem was he couldn't decide the scale of the event. Was what the viewers were describing, while awful, only neighborhood local or was it bigger? What was the cause? There were a lot of ways it could have nothing to do with the terrorism he had immediately envisaged.

He got up from the desk in his library and put on a leather jacket and got a scarf; it was getting colder. As he got out on the street he noticed the leaves were turning, and when he arrived at the lab and Karen met him, the first thing she said was, "I've just turned it on for the first time and something is not working properly about the furnace. It keeps going off and on."

The two of them went down to the basement. As they moved through the house, Michael asked, "So you're pregnant?"

"Yeah. I really want to thank you, Michael, for giving me the two weeks off. Jeff and I are going back to Chillicothe. He's never spent any time with my parents; they only really had a chance to connect at the wedding."

"Good move. I think they'll like him, I certainly do. Is this his last year in medical school? Can I help you all with anything?"

"Thank you, Michael, you're so sweet; I really appreciate it. It has meant… your support…. It has meant a lot to us, to know you were there."

"It has been my pleasure, Karen. You both have made real contributions to the success of the Hill Center. You've been there and I knew I could depend upon you."

Michael rattled the handle of the furnace, and as he did so Karen said, "You know, I wonder whether the explosion

Tracy saw could be caused by a build up of gas or a leaking gas main?"

"I've been thinking about that, and you may be right. All the remote viewers report the debris as coming towards them at an oblique angle...

"Well if that's true, if it was a furnace or gas leak it must be coming from the school towards the lab."

As Michael held the furnace room door open, Karen looked down the hallway that was lined with books.

"Maybe Barbara could help," Karen said, as they walked up the stairs

"I had the same idea. I'm going to talk with her when she gets back."

"Oh, before I forget. Barbara called. She said you volunteered to pick her up at Dulles tomorrow. She gets in on flight 463. I'll put it on your calendar."

"Thanks," Michael said as he fiddled with the furnace. Fifteen minutes later it still didn't work right, and he gave up. As they turned to leave Karen said, "I'll call the furnace people and ask them to send someone out."

"Good," Michael told her, as he continued up the stairs to his office. When he got there he sat down and thought about what Karen had said. He got up again, put on his coat and went back downstairs, waved at Karen, who was on the phone, saying, "I'll be back in a few minutes."

He walked around the corner to the Immaculate Heart School. Fred Dover, an elderly Black man, was wintering roses in beds along the front of the school.

"Fred, I know people who don't get taken care of that well," Michael said.

"How ya doin' Professor. Did you ever get rid of those aphids?"

"Thanks to your magic liquid, my roses both at the lab and at home are bug free," Michael responded with a smile.

"Have you been working the coffee grounds and egg shells into the soil?"

"I have, and even Barbara says there may be hope. She asked me to thank you."

"Wouldn't argue with that."

Michael looked up at the school for a moment, then asked, "Fred, what kind of furnace does the school have?"

"You'd ask me that a month ago, I'da said the bomb kind. Old as the building. But Sister Anne got some banker from Minnesota to give us an entirely new heating and air conditioning plant, including a safety system. It's as nice as you could want. You wanta see it?"

"Naw. I've got to run. Thanks again for the aphid stuff."

"You come see me after the winter, say March. On March 10th. I've got Senator Claiborne and Judge Schneider coming then. Gonna do this once for all of you" Fred said, turning back to his roses. "Can't stand to see grown men torturing perfectly good garden flowers..."

"Thanks Fred, I'll be there."

Michael turned to leave. As he did so he saw a young girl leaving the school, hurried along by a very tough looking man. Instead of walking back around the block, he ran up the stairs as Fred looked after him.

He went into the school and up the stairs, stopping at a door marked, "Headmistress," and knocked.

"Come in," a woman's voice said, and he went in and saw Sister Anne, the headmistress of the school.

"Professor Gillespie. How nice to see you." Noticing Michael's agitation, she added, "Is something the matter?"

"I just saw one of your girls leave with a man who looked, well, sort of threatening. He sort of rushed her into a limo...

"Oh.. I see. Well, thank you for your concern. That was Fatima, probably; the man was her bodyguard. I regret we have come to that... but we have, and we must make the best of it. Several of the girls have bodyguards. Usually, their fathers are diplomats."

"But she's... the man was clearly a Middle Eastern... a Muslim."

Sister Anne smiled at Michael, "Even Muslims want their children to be well educated, Michael. We have a number of Muslim girls. Their fathers appreciate the quality of our pedagogy, and I think they like that we are a single gender school, and are strict about clothing and behavior."

"Oh, I see. Sorry.... I should have thought more," Michael responded, looking rather sheepish, then asked, "Have you ever had a terrorist threat?"

"Twice. It was awful. The girls never knew. Both times we treated it like a fire drill. Thank heavens we were able to keep it out of the papers." The turn of the conversation had made Sister Ann uncomfortable, and she moved to end it, "Thank you again for your concern. I'm sorry, I'm rather busy right now. Is there anything else?"

"No, nothing. Sorry to have burst in on you like this," Michael said, his embarrassment in his voice.

He left Sister Anne's office and went back down the stairs and out onto the sidewalk, waved at Fred and walked back to his lab. As he went along he wondered, if it wasn't the school's furnace, could it really be a terrorist event the viewers saw?

Was it just coincidence that he had chosen that day and time as the target period for the remote viewing sessions? Or had he experienced his own precognition in choosing a date that would produce that result?

He knew from long experience that both the viewer and the monitor were linked, and that the intentions and expectations of each played a role. There was no such thing as an arm's length researcher. It worked best when both held a common intention, that was the ritual importance of the tasking statement. He also knew from the data that highly numinous targets, things that evoked a strong emotional response or were iconic, were easier to remote view.

The more he thought about it, the more he realized he had to put aside for the moment how he acquired the information, the remote viewing part. The real question was: what was his responsibility? What was the correct action? Inside of that he suddenly understood that it was not just his call. This was something they would have to do together, as a team.

As soon as Michael got back into his office, he went through his emails and realized most of the Hill Center people felt the same way he did, and he put out an invitation to everyone inviting them to come to the Center to openly discuss what they should do.

CHAPTER SEVENTEEN

14 November — Washington, D.C. —

Michael pulled up to the curb of Dulles airport fifteen minutes ahead of schedule. He parked in a restricted spot and put Barbara's handicap license on his mirror. He got her traveling wheelchair out of the back, and pushed it across the lot and through the tunnel into the airport's interior, remarking as he did every time he came out to Dulles that there was no other airport like it. Dulles was an architectural interpretation of the wing of the Wright Brothers' biplane.

He went up to the arrivals level and over to where the elevator came down. He didn't have long to wait before Barbara came rolling down the ramp, pushed by a middle aged Hispanic woman who brought her over so she could transfer into her own chair.

"There you are, my darling. The plane was not to be believed. Four teams of cheerleaders..."

Suddenly spilling down the escalator came a swarm of laughing teenage girls in their uniforms. They waited for their baggage with Michael and Barbara, who followed them out to the parking lot where they got aboard two buses and drove off.

Michael pushed Barbara down to his jeep and lifted her aboard, then folded the chair and put it in the back. They had done it many times before.

"So, my darling, what's been happening in my absence?"

"First, tell me what the conference at Cal Tech covered..." Michael answered in part because he wasn't sure how to answer Barbara's question.

He listened and asked questions as they drove back into city down the George Washington Parkway to the Key Bridge in Georgetown, up M Street to 36th, and then to the lab. Michael pulled into the brick terrace laid for this purpose by the Hill Foundation and got Barbara out and into her wheelchair. He used the gentle ramp that led down to the building's lower entrance, and wheeled her down the hall to her apartment that took up the whole back of the house.

It was a custom built combination office and apartment, a complex larger than one might expect, and entirely set up all at one level for a person in a wheelchair. There was a short corridor, with a small kitchen to the left and a bedroom to the right. The main room had a large blackboard on the right wall and a fireplace on the left, and a lima bean shaped desk with multiple screens on it.

The room was cluttered with papers and books, as were the bookcases that lined all the walls with breaks for pictures. A table behind the couch and the end tables next to two comfortable chairs were filled with silver frames containing pictures. The Dalai Lama, Prince William, Barack Obama, Elon Musk, Stephen Hawking and other scientists, a few movie stars, Weldon, and Michael. In one of the breaks between bookcases, there were framed colored drawings by children.

At the back of the room French doors opened out into a small conservatory with comfortable bamboo furniture whose cushions were covered in flowered slip covers. Through the windows at the back of the conservatory a brick terrace and an elegant Georgetown walled garden could be seen.

Carefully tended rose bushes and other plants lined beds along the sides and across the back. A mulberry tree arched over the right back corner of the garden.

Michael helped Barbara transfer again, this time from her folding wheelchair to her motorized one. As she moved she wound down her recounting of the conference saying, "I have to talk to Abrahamson at NSF; you wouldn't believe the mischief Hay has done this time... it will run into dinner. How about we pick this up later this evening, after I get back. You still haven't told me what's new at your end."

"I'll be here," Michael said, and turned to leave, closing the door behind him. He went up the stairs and into his office, and looked through the data from the Vision Probe sessions yet again. There was consensus, and the biometrics and past performance data strongly suggested the information was accurate. Both he and Gilbert had agreed on that before he left for Vancouver. But what was it? And what should they do about it? He still didn't know.

Barbara returned earlier than expected and parked her specially equipped van in on the brick patio the city had permitted the center to build for her personally. A perk for which she was very grateful.

She went into her apartment and took the small elevator which had been built just big enough for her chair. Barbara had introduced Michael to the Hill family, several of whose sons and one daughter had studied under her. She was on their funding committee and supported Michael's grant application. The family had purchased the house and given it to the center knowing that Barbara would live there. The apartment had been created specifically with her needs in mind.

She got off at Michael's floor and rolled down the hall to his office where he sat looking into the fireplace, obviously lost in thought.

"Okay my dear. I realized as I was talking to Albert that you didn't tell me a thing, and encouraged me to go on long past what I know is your interest level in physics politics. So what's going on?"

Michael explained that he had come across something very interesting. He had to be careful what he said, because he wanted Barbara to do a session, and he didn't want to cue her or feed her any information that would pollute her own perceptions. Finally he said, "How about scheduling a session tomorrow?"

"How about scheduling it right now?"

"Would you be up for that? I know you're an owl but…"

"Now would be perfect. Tomorrow I have to go into the lab and I will be swamped."

"Then let's do it," Michael said, getting up, and Barbara went to the elevator and got aboard, while he walked down to the egg. As soon as they were settled they both sat in meditation for twenty minutes. Then Michael began with the usual logon and tasking statement. As Barbara took her breaths with her eyes closed he said, "O.K. Barbara, I want you to move forward in time to 3 p.m. on the 28th of November. You are life sized, and you are on the balcony upstairs looking out. Would you please give me your sense impressions."

"Uhmm… Nothing. Hard to get hold of… Give me the target again…"

"Go forward in time to the 28th of November. It is three p.m."

"Heat. Intense heat. Violent winds. Oh my God. This is... like an explosion. An enormous explosion. Light. Oh... God... Michael," she said, and began to sketch what she saw on her tablet.

"I'm standing looking up at the lab. The blast is coming at my face on the quarter. I feel a tremendous pressure on my body. Odd, there's not as much debris as... Michael I have to stop."

Barbara's entire body shivered. The protocol of the experiment was forgotten. She looked at the sketch she had made, and began to type into her tablet as Michael sat in silence.

"Michael, has anyone else seen anything like this? Come on, my dear, is this why you were so anxious to have me do this viewing? Let me see their results. You have mine. The chronology's intact."

Michael keyed in instructions, the room dimmed, and he showed her the sessions one by one.

"Leave me alone, my dear, and project my tablet on the big monitor. Then go get me a cup of tea. If there is one of Connie's blueberry muffins, that would be lovely too. Make yourself busy. Let me see what I can do." Michael went out of the egg and into the kitchen where he heated water and brewed Barbara's favorite Lapsang Souchong tea mix. In the refrigerator one lone blueberry muffin remained. He cut it in half and put it in the toaster baker oven, then put it on a plate with a smear of butter and took it all back to the egg. Barbara was completely immersed, so he set it down next to her, and went out again and up to his office where he called Tracy.

She wasn't there, and when her voicemail came on he said, "Tracy, I'm sorry I missed you. Barbara did the viewing a few minutes ago. It could be telepathic of course... I've done other sessions... but her vision was almost as forceful as yours. She asked for all the data and is in the egg calculating it now. I just wanted to let you know you're not crazy, I don't think you were hallucinating, and... I love you."

He hung up, surprised at himself for what he had just said.

He went back down to the egg where Barbara was projecting Weldon's drawing and her own superimposed over it. He sat down and quietly watched her. Without saying a word, he knew not to interrupt, he watched as she ate the last bite of the muffin and drank the last of her tea. After another ten minutes she looked up at him. "Michael. I find this hard to believe, but I think that in twenty three days from today, at three p.m., Washington, D.C. will experience a violent explosion, possibly nuclear, whose epicenter will be about fifteen miles east of the lab. If I had to guess its size, I would say about 5 kilotons -- what we call a theater weapon. It will probably explode near the ground, but not on it."

"Nuclear? Couldn't it be something like a gas main?"

"I considered that. But the force... the fact that every viewer reports things moving parallel to the ground not upwards, argues for an explosion some distance away; but for things to move that way requires enormous force. Nuclear... a judgment call... the heat and intense light... again seen by all viewers. Nuclear also because it would take truckloads of conventional explosives, and I can't imagine a scenario where such a quantity would be allowed anywhere near Washington. I ruled out the Navy yard and some kind of accident there because of the blast direction."

"My God. What do we do Barbara? I've been struggling with how to explain a gas main explosion or a conventional terrorist attack. I mean, what do you do when you know about a disaster twenty-three days in advance, but the source of your information is a vision? I don't think we should say anything about this until we know more."

"I agree. We need more data."

Tracy came into the egg as they were talking but didn't overhear them, nor understand the look they exchanged. She walked over and kissed Michael. Barbara took that in but said nothing.

"I just came by to say that Keith has told me he is going to his cousin's for Thanksgiving, so I am happy to accept your invitation."

"Wonderful," Michael said, his face lighting up, and then becoming serious,

"Are you two all right? You don't seem all right?" Michael asked.

Tracy changed the subject, by saying, "You both look very serious. What's going on?"

"Barbara got something very similar to what you saw, Tracy."

Tracy hugged herself, as if feeling a chill, "I don't know how to feel about that, honestly. Confirmed, or scared. Maybe both. I know this sounds so mundane given this, but I have to run. The sitter has an early class," Tracy said and left.

When she was gone, Michael and Barbara went up to Michael's office and went over the data yet again, and she showed him how she had arrived at her conclusions. As she was finishing Barbara said, "I think we should say nothing about this. We're still not sure. I want to do some further calculations and make some other investigations. We need to be as normal in our routines as possible. This could start a panic. So, normal, right?"

"Easy to say...," Michael responded.

"Yeah. Easy to say."

CHAPTER EIGHTEEN

14 November — Mouth of the Ware River, Gloucester, Virginia —

The sailboat Carpe Diem, manned by the Korean couple, was moored to a large duck blind, a sort of free-standing balcony on stilts about ten feet out of the water at the mouth of the Ware, a broad tidal river. The couple, dressed as if out of a catalog, had been picnicking in the blind and were just finishing up. They could not have looked more like autumn cruisers. Affluent Asians cruising the historic tidal rivers of the lower Chesapeake Bay. Warm days but a chill in the air at night; great sailing weather. The man glanced at his watch as he was cleaning up.

"We must be out of here by fifteen hundred," he said, packing away a thermos. He spoke in Korean with an odd formality, and his pronunciation was the dialect of Pyongyang, not Seoul.

"We're going back to Hampton?" the woman asked, in the same accent.

"Those are our orders," he responded.

The man climbed carefully down the ladder to the deck of the boat below. The woman passed things down to him.

"That's everything, " she said as she climbed down.

They went below and stowed the picnic things, then came back out and stepped out of the cockpit onto the deck and went forward to where the orange buoy was lashed to the top of the cabin. Working together, they got it down and took it across to the ladder. The man climbed up first while the woman lashed a line to the buoy and handed it up to the man. As he climbed he pulled up on the line while the woman pushed from below, and together they got the buoy through the small hole into the blind.

The woman went back and began pulling in the side bumpers.

"How long can we stay in the United States?" the woman asked.

"It will take two days to get back, and we have a day in Newport News before we fly out. Didn't they brief you on this?"

"No. I was told to fly down from Philadelphia, meet you and that I was your wife."

"It must have been because you knew how to sail. Where did you learn?"

"I went to the agency school. The same place I learned English. That's where I did my training. I volunteered when they offered a sailing course."

"I see. It has been a pleasure working with you, and we can enjoy the two days back." The man climbed back up the ladder into the blind, holding a spray bottle and some rags. Once inside the blind he looked around, then at his watch. He took the spray bottle and carefully wiped every surface in the blind. Then he climbed back down, wiping surfaces as he went.

As he put the bottle away in a locker under the cockpit seating, he said, "The sea and the air would probably have done it, but now I am sure."

When both were settled in the cockpit, the man started up the engine while the woman went to the bow and untied the boat. The man carefully backed away from the blind until they were about 100 yards off from it. He killed the engine and both of them raised the sails, which caught the wind, heeling the boat over as they sailed out into Mobjack Bay. Half an hour later, when they were just on the horizon, a sport fisherman with a flying bridge came out of the Ware River's mouth and headed towards the blind.

CHAPTER NINETEEN

21 November — Washington, D.C. —

With White House authorization and support from the FBI, Homeland Security, NSA, and DIA, a special projects operations team under Sam Kassimir had set up an operations center dedicated to one thing: finding the warhead before it was used. With 25 years of experience in special operations, Kassimir knew that if they were going to be successful it was essential that there had to be no media leaks. Nothing to alert anyone. No phone calls to reporters, no emails, no tweets, no drinks, no dinners with reporters.

He had made it clear to all of them that if there was even a hint that a 5 kiloton nuclear warhead was loose somewhere in the United States, there would be panic. In his mind he could see the videos on CNN, MSNBC, or FOX. To keep it as secret as possible, Kassimir had arranged to transfer all personnel to Homeland Security, operating under their umbrella, and arranged to house his command center on neutral ground in a warehouse in a secure GSA-maintained building in a complex of maintenance buildings in Crystal City, Virginia. Putting it together had been unlike anything Kassimir had experienced in all his years of special operations. He told a team of engineers what he wanted and it just happened. No forms, no requisitions, no oversight at all.

At the same time he told his people that although they came from different agencies within the team, there had to be absolute candor with no bias for special interests. They had to be intentionally sensitive to anything that might speak to the problem.

Their command center was housed in a SKIF, a Sensitive Compartmented Information Facility. As it played out this meant two metal shipping containers linked together, their size and shape dictated by the fact they had to be capable of being airlifted by helicopters. They were built for much the same purpose, but much larger than the Hill Center's egg, although not as sophisticated. SKIFs took no biometric data, but like the egg were proof against electronic surveillance or output. Being inside was rather like being on a warship, with lots of internal electronics, work cubicles, a head, a small galley, all self-contained when the SKIF was operational. The SKIF's connection with the outer world was a masterful array of cut-outs, making monitoring impossible.

Kassimir had brought with him his original team, now all on temporary open-ended duty assignments, TDYs. Leonard Belmore, Herbert Waterman, and Stanley Potter had become his principal deputies, as well as becoming his friends. The three of them were sitting in the little stainless steel galley area having a morning cup of coffee.

"Are you sleeping well at night?" Waterman asked. They looked at each other, and it was obvious all of them were frustrated and on edge.

"No."

"Me neither. I keep waking up, wondering where the damn thing is."

"Is it in the United States? That's what I keep asking myself," Potter said.

As they sat talking, their tablets beeped; someone on the SKIF intranet.

"Sam wants us," Belmore said.

The all got up and went down to Kassimir's office at one end of the SKIF.

Kassimir looked harassed. His normally heavy beard, unshaved for two days because he had not been home, was even heavier than usual. There were circles under his eyes.

Eventually there were eight people in the room, representing as many agencies.

"The emergency level just went higher, if that's possible" he said. "I called this meeting because I think we are entering the end game. The warhead is in the United States."

"How do we know that?" a sharp-faced woman with dark hair, who represented the NSA, asked.

Kassimir gestured to a man halfway down the table. Andrew Yang, a Chinese American representing ICE, sat up. "We intercepted a North Korean couple in Hampton, Virginia."

"How do you know they are North Korean?" Waterman asked.

"It's funny. Initially it was just a good cop's instinct. There was something artificially perfect about them that caught the attention of one of our men at the Newport News airport. The agent just had a hunch."

"What do you mean... too perfect?" Potter asked.

Yang thought for a moment, "He said it was like watching a magazine ad. Just the right shoes, the right clothes with the right jewelry, glasses, luggage. They stood out. In fact, at first he thought they were shooting a commercial."

Denzel Hammer was the Homeland Security representative, a very fit looking African American with a razor cut. He picked up the thread. "We were notified and picked them up for questioning. Usual routine. We put them in a room and let them sit for several hours while we live streamed a video of them to a research lab we fund. They watched the couple when they were alone together. They didn't say much, which told us they were well-trained; but they did have to agree to a common story, and we caught the accent when they were not "on" in front of people. It's North Korean. Also the physiology people who looked at the data are sure they're not married, although the paperwork says they are."

"Yes," Yang added. "The psychology people thought the same. They looked like they were playing a part. As we held them we searched, and the paperwork fell apart four iterations out."

"What have they said?" Tom Johnson asked. He was a man in his mid-forties with a surprisingly anonymous face, who represented the FBI.

"Under some duress," the Homeland security man said, "they admitted that they had picked something up and left it in a duck blind in the Chesapeake Bay, believe it or not. Down near the Hampton Roads."

"But we don't think they actually knew what it was. They just did what they were told," Yang explained.

"The problem," Kassimir said, "is that no interrogation technique, even the nasty ones, are going to buy us time. If the bomb is in Virginia, and it was dropped off above the Hampton Roads naval basin, that may be because surveillance is much tighter in the Hampton Roads due to all the secure facilities. The idea may be to take it back down by truck or car."

"Or bring it north, up here, a few hours drive," Belmore added.

"Exactly. Either way, gentlemen and ladies, I think that if we don't catch it this bomb is going to go off in a few days, and if it is headed our way the world may change within the week."

"Why do you think the Koreans had it? Couldn't they just be ordinary spies?" the NSA woman asked.

"We think they were involved because they came to the U.S., rented a sailboat in Miami and went to sea. We know they crossed over to the Bahamas, came back, and were sailing up to the East Coast because they were stopped by a Customs boat. We know they picked something up and dropped it off. What else could it be?" Kassimir asked, and looked around the table.

"Why would two North Koreans rent a sailboat to sail up the East Coast in early fall?" the preppy looking man representing DIA said, not as a question but a statement.

"That's the question. We don't know the answer."

A rather elegant woman in her fifties, who represented the Asian section at CIA, had been silent until then but now spoke up. "There is a rumor we think makes sense. A bomb was stolen in Turkmenistan; it was taken somewhere and disassembled. Just the warhead, stripped of its electronics, casing and all that, has been moving west. We are pretty sure an SAS team in Ireland almost got it, and that it had come from a country that spoke Arabic," the woman explained.

"Thanks, Patricia," Kassimir said. "We have never seen anything like this. Every terrorist movement in the world seems to have participated in this."

"Where did these Koreans get the bomb from?" Waterman asked.

"We don't know."

"You picked them up in Virginia. Why were they there?" Johnson asked.

"They turned in their sailboat in Hampton; it was a bareboat charter," Yang responded.

Kassimir looked around the table, watching each of them absorb the briefing. He could see it had gone from being an abstraction, like a drone strike in Afghanistan, to something very personal. If the bomb was headed towards Washington, they all lived in or around the city; their families, their children were in the D.C. area.

"Whatever you can do… do it," Kassimir said, and stood up. "Time is running out." The others stood, and except for Belmore, Waterman, and Potter, they all walked out of the SKIF.

When they were gone Kassimir and the other three stood for moment.

"What do you think the chances are?" Belmore asked the group.

"Right now I think we are going to experience a nuclear event within the week. Once they get this, wherever it is heading, they're going to set it off. They're not going to wait; that would just up the risk of discovery. That's what I think," Kassimir said.

"I agree," Waterman responded. "They're going to know, when the Koreans don't get back, that we're on to it. They must know we will do whatever we can to find it. So what's the upside of hanging onto it?"

CHAPTER TWENTY

21 November — Washington, D.C. —

"Hurry, Sarah, or we're going to be late," Tracy said to her daughter who was bent over a piece of paper on their dining room table, finishing her painting of a turkey.

"Just a minute, Mommy. I'm finishing my painting for Thanksgiving."

A few minutes more and Sarah was finished. She got up and ran to her room, got out her new black dress-up shoes and put them on, carefully buckling the little straps across her feet. She went out of her room and found her mother waiting with her best dress-up coat. She put it on then ran over to the table, tested to see the paint was dry on the paper, and rolled her watercolor into a tube.

"Come on Sarah, we have to go," Tracy said, growing impatient, putting on her own coat. They left the apartment and walked the few blocks to Michael's house, with Sarah holding the rolled up painting under her arm.

"This is a big people's party," Sarah said as Michael's house came into view. "Will there be any other children?" she asked, looking up at her mother.

"I don't know," Tracy responded. "These are all people from the lab, and I don't know all of them yet, my love," Tracy answered.

"I always like Professor Gillespie's house," Sarah said, opening the white gate.

"Why's that, dear?"

"It's smaller than the others," Sarah answered, indicating the brick houses on either side. "I like the plants and the flowers," she added.

"So do I," Tracy said, looking down and smiling.

They knocked on the door and after a moment Michael answered.

"Come in," then looking down and smiling at Sarah, he said, "And I am so glad you brought Sarah."

"Keith…" Tracy began, but Michael waved the comment away.

In the living room, Weldon, Barbara, Karen, Coyote, Constance, and partners she had never met, stood with wine glasses in hand in animated conversations. A vaporizer was being passed around. She said hello to the room, then introduced her daughter.

"This is Sarah."

"What do you have there, under your arm?" Constance asked.

In response Sarah unrolled her picture of a turkey.

"Do you think this is big enough to feed everyone?" Michael asked her.

Sarah grabbed Michael's arm, saying, "Don't be silly, that's a paper turkey!" Everyone laughed.

Weldon got up from his chair and came over, taking the painting from Michael. "Hey, Professor! Don't you know a work of art when you see one? Follow me, Sarah, I know exactly where this should go."

Sarah followed Weldon as he stepped over to a table filled with food, a well roasted turkey at its center. He took a small picture off the wall behind the table, and set it on the sideboard. Where the nail was, he pushed the paper with the turkey painting so it was now hanging on the wall above the turkey. Everyone applauded, and Sarah felt delighted. Then they all sat down and began to eat.

Tracy found herself next to Constance.

"It's like a family, but not quite that; we're a tribe."

"Yes. But there is more than that." Constance answered. "If I were writing it as a paper, I would say Hill Center was a school for shamans." As Constance took that in, Tracy asked, "H ow did you get interested in this?"

"My mother was interested in Edgar Cayce."

"I don't know who that is."

"Oh, he's been dead for years. He was a kind of remote viewer, just extraordinarily gifted. He gave thousands of readings, sessions as we would say, and they were all meticulously documented by a woman named Gladys Davis. All the records, everything she could track down. Like our experiments, there was an unimpeachable chronology. Like us there was no possibility that Cayce could know the information he gave. Anyway, growing up that was part of my life. My mother belonged to a Search for God Cayce Study Group. Oh, could you pass the gravy," Constance said, then thanked her when she did.

"When I went away to Howard—that's where I did my undergraduate work—I went to a group on campus once and I met Herbert there," Constance said, looking across the table to her husband who was deep in conversation with Karen's husband, Jeff.

"How long have you been together?"

"Twenty-eight years. We have two boys, both grown. One's in the air force, the other is on a research vessel somewhere in the Pacific Northwest. Sarah's your first?"

"Yes, she's seven.

"I hope you don't mind my asking," Constance said, leaning towards Tracy. "I've heard you are going through a hard divorce."

"You've heard right," Tracy said putting down her fork. "Part of it is because of what we are all doing, why we all know each other."

"Not open to facts, I assume," Constance said, putting her hand on Tracy's.

"No. Not at all... yet he prides himself on being a rational fact-based person."

"Herbert's brother, Edward, is like that. He's a fundamentalist, and an accountant, and thinks I'm satanic, although he won't say it to my face. It's like a sore that never fully heals."

"I am beginning to understand that. Oh, Constance is that what I am going to have to deal with while Sarah is growing up?"

The two women looked at one another, turned and hugged. Then they laughed and went back to eating.

At the other end of the table Michael and Coyote had finally found some time together.

"I went back to the res, Michael."

"You're from Old Oraibi aren't you?"

"That's right. You remembered."

"I have always been interested in the Hopi. Your beliefs about consciousness agree with much of what I have learned doing research."

"You know I told you, you were the first White man I ever met who seemed to understand my world view."

The two men went back to eating for moment, then Coyote said, "Cheveyo, our chief, and I talked when I went home. I had told him before what I was doing with you, and he asked me how it was going."

"What did you say?"

"I told him that I thought what I was doing was the equivalent of a vision quest, just in the White world's scientific way."

Michael burst out laughing, and several people looked his way before going back to their own conversation.

"You're right. Tracy thinks that as well. So do I. Do you know the Kogi?"

"No, who are they?"

"I think you would probably see them as cousins," Michael said. "The Kogi – it means jaguar in their language – are an indigenous people who live in an unusually remote and isolated mountain range that runs through the Sierra Nevada de Santa Marta. The Sierra Nevada is the world's highest coastal mountain range. They live quite consciously choosing to remain apart from the general Columbian culture. They believe that one of the mountains in the range, Pico Cristóbal Colón, is "The Heart of the World," and that they are the "elder brothers" and the others outside their culture are the "younger brothers."

"To guide their culture, the Kogi have developed a shamanic nonlocal consciousness corps called Mamas. The Kogi identify certain male children at birth and put them in a cave system where they spend the first nine years of their lives, attended only by their mother and the priests. They are taught deep meditation and focusing techniques that open them to nonlocal consciousness, which they characterize as a Great Mother they call Aluna. When the boys are brought out of the cave and introduced into the larger culture, their role is to open to the nonlocal and report what they see about the future, or individuals, or the community."

"We don't do that, but I get that we're both cultures based on consciousness," Coyote said.

"That's why I know about your culture, the strong tradition of training people to open to the nonlocal. Look at chanting and a few cups of water to grow the blue corn, when it should not be able to grow at all. That requires linking with the matrix of consciousness."

"You know about that?" Coyote said. "I'm surprised. But yes."

"It's a recurring theme across culture, time, and geography. A lot of cultures develop systems, institutions to train people to open to the nonlocal: the temple attendants at the Delphic Oracle in Greece, the Talking Idol of Sihwa — a specially trained temple attendant speaking through a physical idol— in Egypt, or the Mayan oracle, The Talking Idol of Ix Chel, on the Mexican island of Cozumel," Michael said, picking up a fork of stuffing.

"And at the Hill Center you've put together the White man's version," Coyote said as a statement.

"Not quite," Michael answered. "The science version, all races and ethnicities are welcome, and religion as dogma is not a component, although it can be a teacher. The shamanic rituals your people developed empirically over centuries, in my world are protocols. What we do here at Hill in your world is ritual, wouldn't you agree?" Michael asked.

"Exactly. That's why this is the only place I feel really comfortable. I know that in the night world I am... lit. But I'm still an outsider," Coyote said, and looked down very thoughtfully. Michael just waited. Then Coyote began again, "It wasn't until right now that I understood why. I don't feel like an outsider when I'm with the Hill tribe. That's how I think of us," Coyote said, looking at Michael. "It's not physical things that make the cultures different. It's consciousness."

"Yes," Michael answered.

"You are such a trip," Coyote said. "Now I understand why Cheveyo is doing this, and I hope he will let me sit in on your conversations. He is inviting you to come and join us for the Kachina ceremonies that are coming up. I don't think I have ever seen a White man in the kiva during the ceremonies."

"I accept. Tell him I am honored."

"I'll introduce you to him by email, and you can tell him yourself. He also Skypes," Coyote said with a laugh, then serious again he added, "This is a big deal in my world, Michael."

"It's a big deal in mine," Michael replied. "By the way, what does Cheveyo mean?"

"Spirit Warrior."

As he said that, both noticed that people were getting up and clearing the table. A subgroup took on doing the washup; Michael's kitchen was too small for a lot of people. The rest went back into the living room for coffee and liqueurs. They were all just settling when the doorbell rang.

Michael got up and when he opened the door Keith was standing there. "Hello, Keith. Come in."

Keith came only a short way into the front hall, ignoring Michael's proffered hand.

Michael turned toward the kitchen and called out, "Sarah, your dad is here."

She ran into the room and over to her father, giving him a big hug. He picked her up.

"Oh...Daddy. I got to pull the wishbone and I won..."

"Glad to hear somebody did. Get your coat, Sarah."

Tracy came into the room and took Sarah's coat out of the closet and helped her on with it.

"Hi Keith." Then, to Sarah, "What a lucky girl. You're going to have two Thanksgivings today."

"Spare us the forced humor, Tracy."

"Keith, please...."

"We're not going to fight. I'm just going to take my daughter and get out of here. Come on Sarah..."

Sarah sensed the tension between her parents and began to sniffle, upset by their cold words.

Michael came into the hall and said, "Keith, for God's sake. Let's not make this any harder..."

"Thanks for the advice. Let's go Sarah." He took his daughter's hand and left the house, leaving a room silent with embarrassment for Tracy. It broke the evening's mood, and shortly afterward several of the other guests left as well. Finally, only Michael, Tracy, Barbara and Weldon remained.

"Nothing seems to be goin' right," Weldon said, putting plates back into the cupboard. "I got hired to paint a house last week and when I showed up yesterday with the paint the wife had picked out, the husband had returned from a trip. He hated the color... they got into a fight... an' I lost the job. They paid for the paint, but what am I gonna do with it? Know anyone who needs six gallons of Magenta Sunset..." His words lifted the mood, and they all laughed.

Tracy, leaning against Michael's butcher block counter, said, "It's funny how the world you think is in place in a certain way suddenly isn't that way at all."

"Speaking of which, I've got something I need to tell you," Michael said, putting down his dishtowel. He looked at Barbara, "I think you are right. We'll go that way." Then to the rest of them "No... show you would be better. I'd like you all to go to the lab with me."

"Now?" Tracy asked.

"Yes. I've been thinking about this all day. It's important or I wouldn't ask. Let's finish up and go to the lab. We don't have to hurry, but after we're through."

Ten minutes later they were putting on their coats. Weldon helped Barbara with her electric wheelchair, and they were soon moving down the brick sidewalks of Georgetown.

They arrived at the Hill Center and went up to the second floor to the conference room opposite Michael's office. He walked to the front and activated the projection system. But before projecting anything, he said, "You all know good experimentation calls for blind protocols... I don't know what the answer is... and neither do you, as a viewer. We're into new territory. But in this case it's no longer a question of researcher and viewer. I can't make the decisions that need to be made by myself. And I can't tell everyone at the lab, or we would have no viewers. So I want to ask you to cross over to my side of the bio-circuit and help me."

Then he projected images and the transcribed words of each session as the biometric data scrolled along beneath the the viewers' drawings.

"Look at this description of Tracy's. That's where we begin."

"Note the comment about heat, strong light, and the wind." He called up the next screen, "Here's John Sacks' session. Notice the heat light motif."

"John's an interior designer. I see what you mean that the skills sets we have in regular life carry over into the nonlocal. His 'hit' rate is off the charts about the design of things," Tracy observed.

"Yes, in the same way that you are particularly attuned, to cultural nuance and mannerisms," Michael responded. "You don't get stupid in nonlocal awareness."

"Yes, but less rational."

"Exactly. Here's Connie's. Same elements. Note also across them all there is a clear sense of the direction the wind is coming from. That's important because it gives us a vector for the explosion." Then another image appeared. "Weldon... here's yours. Once again the same elements."

The images were lined up across the screens as Michael said, "It is a very large explosion, and its blast wave is still violently hot and fast at the point we experience it. There is too much consistency here for it all to be just... mental noise. I believe you all were seeing a real event. The question is, what event?"

"A gas main?" Weldon asked.

"That was my first thought. I also thought of the furnace of the school. But Immaculate Heart has a brand new state of the art climate system paid for by a billionaire in Minnesota. No. I think the evidence is clear it isn't anything like that," Michael said, and turned. "Maybe Barbara should take over from here."

Barbara wheeled herself to the head of the table and Michael sat down. "I believe a large bomb of some kind will be exploded at 3 p.m. on the 28th."

"Bomb. What kind of bomb?" Weldon was a vet; they could see on his face memories of what that meant. "We talkin' war?"

"We don't know, Weldon." She exchanged a look with Michael. "What do you think, Michael?"

"We'll do some lat-long sessions with other viewers looking at other locales. But not with any of you. That's the trouble. By bringing you inside of this, on my side of the experiment equation, you become hopelessly polluted with intellectual information. From now on it would be hard to tell whether what you were seeing was genuine nonlocal perception, or just a recap of what you've mentally learned."

Michael looked around and saw the clear disappointment in each face.

"Okay. I've talked it over with Gilbert, and since it all lies in the future he thinks the biometric record may resolve the conflict, because your body will have psychophysical reactions, and we have a history of response accuracy correlated to the biometrics. But it's new territory. I'll have to treat you as a second population, but let's put that aside for the moment. Barbara isn't finished."

"By calculating the lines of force we have each described," Barbara said, and showed a new image with vectors of force projected, "I have refined my original calculation of fifteen to twenty miles away with a burst point in the air not on the ground. Working first off a map of the city, and then through driving the streets in the area, I think I have identified the specific block and building."

Everyone but Michael, who already knew it, was stunned. "Oh Barbara, that's wonderful. We can call the police and turn the information in…" Tracy said excitedly.

"No, not a cold call," Michael said. "We have to assume nobody knows anything about this. We have to do this differently, but let's put that aside for the moment as well. There's more that Barbara needs to say"

"The bomb is almost certainly nuclear… in the 5 kiloton range."

"A nuclear bomb is going to go off in Washington in seven days. My God, we've got to tell people. Who cares if they think we're crazy… I've got to get Sarah out of the city," Tracy said, and the others nodded in affirmation.

"This is what I've been wrestling with," Michael said, "What do ordinary people do when they know something extraordinary, from a nonlocal perception source, that could change the lives of millions?"

It brought them back to earth and for a moment they sat in silence.

Then Barbara brightened. "Wait a minute. Michael's right; the way to do this is not a cold call to the police. I don't know why I didn't think it. I have a friend… an acquaintance really. A fellow named Jake Garth. He's a member of the intelligence community with whom I've worked on that DOE group. I just thought of him because at the Cal Tech meetings, I discussed my involvement with Michael. Garth was open-minded enough not to scoff. Perhaps, he might be worth a try. I could set up a meeting."

"If you ask at least we'll get a hearing," Michel said, "and it would connect us to a completely different level of government. Give it a try."

Weldon, who had been quiet for quite a while, spoke up. "This is awful hard for me... I've just got to think about this, Michael. I'll call you tomorrow," he said, getting up to leave.

'That's a good idea, Weldon. We all need to think about this," Barbara said. "Will you help me down to my flat?" He smiled and they left together. Michael and Tracy, who were the only ones left, could hear the elevator going down.

"Michael, could we go through the sessions again?"

"Sure. What are you looking for..."

"I don't know. But there was a lot of stuff we didn't include."

"Barb and I thought the same thing, but we went back and forth through it. Most of it seems like mental noise... or stuff we couldn't evaluate. But hell... give it a try."

They went back through the same images and words. When they come to the face of a bald headed bearded man, Tracy stopped.

"What about that? Who drew that?"

"That was Connie. Who knows? Could be anybody or nobody."

"Isn't that one of those low a priori things you're always talking about, something you don't expect?"

"Maybe."

"What about these numbers.. N749"

"That's another one-off...I don't know. I keep thinking they remind me of something..."

"Almost like a ham's call letters. My brother was an amateur radio operator when he was in Boy Scouts. He had numbers like that..."

"I hadn't thought of that, Tracy. You may be on to something."

CHAPTER TWENTY-ONE

23 November — Washington, D.C. —

Tracy looked at her watch and realized she had only a few minutes to get across campus for her appointment with Goldie. The tension between them had reached a point where for several days Tracy had been thinking about ending her therapy. She admired and respected Goldman but they seemed increasingly at cross purposes, so she experienced the sessions less as therapy and more as a forced meeting with a disapproving parent.

She felt guilty because she was going to do something about which Michael would be very unhappy. She was going to show Goldie some of the data, relying on doctor-patient confidentiality.

But the forms held, and when Goldman opened her door and invited her to come in she did, and they both smiled. She sat in her chair for a moment and played aimlessly with a small clip she had found in her pocket, then said, "Well, I know you're not going to be happy about this, but I have kept on with my remote viewing. In fact that's what I want to talk about today. Something has happened."

"You seem very agitated. Do you want to tell me about it?"

"With good reason, Goldie. Let me show you something." Tracy reached into her briefcase, pulled out her tablet, and brought up the drawings from the sessions. She stood up and laid the tablet on the desk. Goldman got up as well, and they stood looking down at them for a moment before asking, "What am I looking at?"

"Each of these drawings was done by a different person on different days, men and women. But each was targeted on the same date and time as I was when I had what you called an hallucination."

"I don't understand."

"Look at the similarities...!" Tracy said with some annoyance in her tone.

"Tracy, I have already told you that the reality of what you call nonlocal perception is improbable to begin with. Even if there were some basis for it, the effect it is having on you frankly alarms me. Your dramatic life-changing actions suggest to me an oncoming crisis. Even if these things were true...and I do not concede that... the issues you face are in your world now, not in some future, and they must be addressed," Goldman said, sitting back down in her chair. "Let me ask you something. How much time is all of this taking?"

"God, it's taking... I can't get it out of my head," Tracy said as she sat down as well. "I mean, if you thought a bomb was going to go off here next week, wouldn't you be concerned?"

"I'm sure I would be if I thought that. But what I see is a person I care about retreating from the difficulties of her life. No...let me ask you. How do you feel about all of this?"

"Frustrated... scared... just what you'd expect."

"That should be your clue. It's time to regroup Tracy. Not go charging off into this... I'm sorry but I have no choice but to consider this a fantasy."

"Do you know Barbara Strickland?"

"The physicist? I don't know her but of course I know of her. Any woman who wins a Nobel in physics can hardly be considered anonymous. What about her?"

Tracy got up again, came over to the desk, and went back through the images until she stopped at one. "This is Barbara Strickland's session. She's also one of the remote viewers in this series. She's also the person who did the analysis about the explosion...."

Goldman was visibly surprised hearing Strickland's name and involvement, but quickly controlled her expression, saying, "Tracy, as much as I respect and admire Professor Strickland, it doesn't change my position. Even if this information is correct, it still is inappropriate in my judgment for you to be involved in this probing of your unconscious."

"This is not about my unconscious, Goldie... at least not in the way you mean. My scientific training is as well-based as yours. Your prejudice is blocking any good I can get from your therapy. I cannot make myself heard."

"You're heard all right, you just confuse hearing with agreement."

Tracy stood up, gathered up her tablet and put it back in her briefcase.

"Thank you for everything you have done, Goldie," Tracy said, putting out her hand. "And I remind you, everything I have told you is within our confidential doctor patient relationship."

"Really, you feel a need to cite that, Tracy," Goldman responded. She took a breath and after a pause, "Why don't you think about it. My door is always open to you. And let me write something for you that will help with your anxiety which

I can see is increasing," Goldman said as she wrote on her prescription pad, tore off the page, and held it up to Tracy.

"No thank you, Goldie. I don't need drugs. My anxiety is well-grounded."

"Just take it," Goldie said, offering it again. This time Tracy accepted the piece of paper.

She left Goldie's office and walked back across the campus to her classroom. She passed a trash bin, wadded up the prescription and threw it into the bin. She felt shaken by the exchange with Goldie, and was willing to admit it to herself. But she knew she had made the right decision.

As Tracy was walking across the campus, Michael was in his office on the phone. "That's right. Dr. Strickland felt it was appropriate... She has already.... Good. Then perhaps you know... I see. When would be a convenient time to get together? Yes there is some urgency. How about the Mikado on Wisconsin? You know it... great. Seven-thirty tonight. I'll see you then." Michael broke the connection and paused for a moment, looking at his phone. The caller had been Jake Garth who, as he said, had called Michael at Barbara's urging. He looked at his watch and went down to the center's classroom to teach a third-year anthropology group. Some were Tracy's students; she had asked him to do a presentation on the neurophysiology of altered states of consciousness. An hour later Karen came to him with a thick list of calls and papers, and that ate up the rest of his day until six-thirty, when he left to meet Garth.

When he got to the Mikado at first he didn't see anyone, but the hostess came and he gave her his name. She told him he was expected and directed him back to a booth off to one side and out of most sight lines. Seated at the table was a man in his forties, a few years older than Michael, with that odd mix of military posture and anonymous federal bureaucrat that Michael had come to recognize as the look of those who inhabited the fringes of science where it met the intelligence and defense world.

He went over, introduced himself, and sat down. They made small talk while sizing each other up, and Michael decided to trust Garth; he was amiable, and seemed genuine. More importantly, Barbara seemed to trust him.

As they ate a dinner of mixed sushi and sashimi, some mentaiko, and a side of seaweed salad, he took looks at Garth and felt his assessment returned. To make conversation they talked about Barbara. About twenty minutes in, after they ordered a second small bottle of sake, they decided to quit small talk and got down to it. Michael took out his tablet and showed Garth the same presentation Tracy had shown Dr. Goldman.

"As weird as it sounds I have reasonable confidence that this explosion really is on the cards. Barbara has charted it to a specific locale. Here, let me show you," Michael said pulling up Google Earth, and pinpointing the location.

"What is the accuracy rate on your experiments?"

Michael moved to another screen and opened copies of other session drawings and observations. "You can search on my name on Academia.edu; you'll find a number of papers that describe the consensus methodology we use. I've written it out in detail, so I won't take your time with that now other than to say it is as rigorous a protocol as I and my critics can make it," Michael said with a laugh. "But, to answer your question directly. Typically about thirty five to forty per cent of the data we get on application studies like this cannot be evaluated,."

"What do you mean?" Garth asked, suddenly alert.

"What someone thought in a particular situation, or what the woman who owned a vase a thousand years ago looked like. The viewer's description might be correct, but there's no way to know, so we call it, 'can't be evaluated.' Then there is a 'partially correct, where a detail may be wrong but everything else is operationally correct."

"What do you mean?" Garth questioned again.

"This is not about incorrect statements; the calibration is incorrect concepts," Michael said but he could see that Garth did not really get his point. So, after finishing a California roll, he continued. "If I say the athletic man wearing a brown tweed jacket sitting in a sushi bar, that's only one sentence. We assess not only by statement, but also by concept, and that's eight concepts… brown, tweed, and jacket. You see what I mean?"

"I get it," Garth said, and Michael could see that he did.

"Of the sixty to sixty-five percent that can be assessed, that is usually done by independent experts who have no other role in the experiment. They're picked for their expertise in certain areas and thus are able to make a much more nuanced assessment then a generalist would. They typically rate concept accuracy to be seventy-five to eighty-five percent correct, or partially correct but still operationally useful. Some viewers reach ninety percent accuracy on some projects, and we are beginning to understand why that happens."

"That's very impressive. You say it is all logged and there is an unimpeachable chronology showing the remote viewing data that was collected prior to the reveal, whatever it is?"

"Oh, yes. Everything is digitally recorded. We also have a full suite of biometric measurements: EEG, respiration, blood pressure. Also voice analysis, facial analysis, the whole nine yards. We build up track records on each viewer, and that plus the biometric data tells us the probability any given concept is going to be correct."

Garth took a bite of mentaiko, chewed and swallowed, then asked, "Are you willing to make this available?"

"To the right people, yes," Michael responded.

Garth dipped another roll in some soy sauce flavored with wasabi and gari and took another bite, using the time to think. Swallowing, he looked at Michael very seriously.

"Okay, tell me the downside of all this."

Michael nodded agreement and started. He had already thought through all of it.

"For starters the very idea of an explosion suggests a bomb, which leads to terrorists and other such formula images. That's typical. Such a scenario also produces an unusual amount of what you might think of as 'noise' in the data... sort of like static on a radio signal. Analytical stuff. Fears. Cultural conditioning. You can see the noise in this obvious sort of generic terrorist face. This bearded guy. I mean, once you start thinking about an explosion every thriller you've ever seen on television or at the movies comes out of your unconscious. Then, there's just plain gobbledy goop stuff... for instance a recurring number sequence that has shown up," Michael said, calling up a page on his tablet, and handing it to Garth. They both pored over it for a moment.

"In several of the sessions," Michael said, and he brought up a page that showed multiple drawings, "several viewers described an old fashioned railroad engine; three of them even drew it. This may be analytic overlay... projections from the viewer's memory about movies with boiler explosions, thus the train. But I could be wrong; this could be dead on. That's the problem we face. The analytical part of the mind always tries to make sense of the intuitive images it gets. But for all that, in every single session the initial virgin image is of an explosion. It's uniform and consistent across all sessions."

Garth sat back in the booth with his cup of tea and took a sip. "I don't pretend to know anything about this subject. And as far as I know there are no nuclear bombs floating around unaccounted for. As you can imagine we pay pretty close attention to such things. But Barbara Strickland is a serious lady... you're pretty well respected yourself... I checked... and I have seen television shows about using psychics to solve crimes. I even have a personal experience. When I was in Afghanistan, a nineteen year-old from Tennessee who had never been out of his state, a private in my platoon, led us to a camp where one of our guys was being held. There was no way he could have known," Garth said, then indicated the tablet. "Can I have that Powerpoint?"

"Sure," Michael answered. "I assumed you would want it. It's on this thumb drive," he said handing it to Garth. "I didn't feel safe sending it over the net.

"Very smart," Garth nodded, taking the drive. "Does this include the man's face? It will help me explain what you mean by 'noise.' Let me talk to some people... sort of feel around. See if there's any interest. I'll get back to you in a few days."

"A few days are all we've got," Michael said, and signaled for the check.

CHAPTER TWENTY-TWO

24 November — Washington, D.C. —

Jake Garth went home from the dinner with Michael, confused. Michael seemed a rational person; he was considered an excellent researcher, the protocol he described was impressive but still, he decided, he would not have paid attention to any of it had it not been for the involvement of Barbara Strickland. Yet what Michael had told him nagged at him and he did not sleep well, finally giving up at three-thirty. Even though it was Sunday, he got up, showered and dressed, and drove into his office, taking Michael's little thumb drive with him. Drawing the data from the drive but not downloading it so that there would be as few sources as possible, he sat down to go through it all again.

At seven sharp he called and told the man at the other end. "I think it's worth the time, or I wouldn't be dragging you out of bed.... quit complaining, I've been up all night... I could've called earlier. He'll call me... all right I'll wait."

He hung up the phone, and once again began to go through the material. After a short wait the phone rang. Garth picked it up on the first ring.

"Yes sir. I believe so, sir," he said without preamble. He listened for a moment and replied, "All right, your home. Yes I know Chain Bridge Road. Gallant Green. Yes, sir. Turn right... I'm at the Pentagon... about 45 minutes. No sir, I have not had breakfast."

He hung up and looked at the phone for a moment, recognizing that he was now committed. He ejected the drive, put it in his pocket and picked up his laptop. At the door he picked up a telephone oddly placed next to the jamb. There was no dial. Adjacent to it was a small box with a button.

"This is Colonel Garth. Four Bravo Four Five Five. The code word for the day is Mercury. I am securing...now" he said as he pressed the button, and turned out the lights. "I am secured. You too, lieutenant," he said, and hung up the phone.

He closed the door and then tapped a code in the box outside his office next to the door. The corridor was empty except midway down where a guard stood at ease in a side corridor that linked the five pentagons nestled one within another. He came briefly to attention as Garth walked by, but the only sound was the tap of Garth's heels.

He went out at the parking level and headed for the GNU section of the vast lot, at the time almost empty, although other sections further away from the building for lower ranking people were fuller. He got into his car and drove off onto the George Washington Parkway, which tracked the Potomac River. It took him out to Mclean, Virginia, where he turned on Gallant Green Road and up a lengthy driveway to a Georgian house situated on manicured grounds.

Garth noticed there were several other cars in the parking area. He got out and, as he did so, the door opened and Kassimir was standing in the entry.

"Come in, Colonel. You look like a man who could use a cup of coffee."

They crossed the living room and went into an enclosed sun porch. Another man in his late 40s, with thinning hair and rimless glasses, was already seated.

"Colonel, let me introduce you to Will Edwards, a nuclear physicist I asked to join us."

"Yes sir. Nice to meet you."

"And you. I understand you have something rather interesting for us."

"To tell you the God's own truth, I don't know what I've got. But I thought I ought to get this to you ASAP."

"Okay," Kassimir said, pressing a button that lowered a screen and turned on a projector.

"You can hook up your laptop here," Kassimir said, pulling out a cable from a tambour next to his chair. "We don't do wireless for security. We'll even feed you for your trouble, when you're through," he said, turning and smiling at Garth.

For the next thirty minutes Garth spoke uninterrupted by the others, and walked them through the images and descriptions Michael had shown him.

When he was finished, Kassimir led the two men into the dining room where an English breakfast was laid out on the buffet. While they ate, Kassimir and Will peppered Garth with questions, most of which he could not answer. Finally, as they were sitting around the table with the devastation of the breakfast spread before them, Garth said, "I wouldn't have brought any of this to you, except Barbara Strickland takes it very seriously, as does the director of the Hill Center, a Professor Gillespie, and another professor, a young anthropologist, Tracy Walsh."

"We take it seriously too, Colonel. We must bring you onto our little team now. From this point on everything we discuss is above Q. You understand. This is the best kept secret in America."

Garth was visibly startled and experienced a kind of frisson.

"Yes sir."

"Why don't you start, Will? You both have your tablets, so hook up and we can look at the evidence together as we talk." After a beat, Will began. "Reports have been coming in for several months that a joint-force drawn from the international terrorist network, combining elements of ISIL, a Libyan-Iraqi faction paid for by a Saudi prince, an Irish group, and some kind of government sanctioned team from North Korea, obtained a five-kiloton nuclear device stolen from a facility in Turkmenistan. For the past several months this group has been moving it into the U.S., where it is now. Other sources have described its deconstruction... alteration really... something that apparently was done in a lab somewhere in the Middle East. We think we know who did it; knowing how to alter nuclear bombs is not a widely spread skillset, but we're not sure."

Jake brought up the drawing Constance had made. "This is the man Gillespie says the viewers describe as the key person... But Gillespie warned it may be nothing. He thinks this may be what he calls analytical overlay. That is, bombs, terrorists, people from the Middle East; it all just flows together, you know. Once you start down that track, maybe this is what you get to, a kind of fantasy. On the other hand, I got the feeling he thinks it is accurate. I think that is kind of interesting because he has no way of knowing any of the things you just told me."

Kassimir looked at the image as Jake spoke, and interrupted, "It's a rather good likeness... what's most interesting is that it shows him as he now appears, after the plastic surgery he doesn't think we know about. That's very interesting. "

"Who is he? Jake asked.

"Basma El Farouk," Will answered. "Syrian-Lebanese background, Harvard undergrad, M.S. and Ph.D. in nuclear physics from MIT. He's the scientist who we think oversaw the alteration using a kryton trigger stolen from a lot sent by Texas Instruments to Europe. Farouk is a serious guy with a serious grudge. The Israelis working with an American mercenary contract operative captured and killed his brother. His family home was bulldozed during the Intafada."

"We create our own enemies," Kassimir said with disgust.

"The clincher, though," Will said, "is your train drawing. The guy's a nut for toy trains. Exact replicas. Old-fashioned steam trains, just like the drawings. Makes them from scratch. What your Professor Gillespie thinks may be, what does he call it, analytical overlay, in fact is so spot on I find it a little scary. What I don't understand," Will continued, "is why this lab came up with this information?"

"I don't know, sir. I suppose it could be something as simple as a coincidence," Jake answered. "The Hill Center people just happened to pick the right time in the right city."

"I don't believe in coincidences... and even if I did... I don't like them," Kassimir replied, turning to Garth.

"You said this man, Gillespie, impressed you as being a good scientist. I suppose he would have to be for Strickland to be involved with him. I am impressed with his thoroughness at least. It seems very competent." Kassimir looked at Garth's tablet. "You say you haven't downloaded this anywhere?"

"No, it's on this SanDisk," he said, extracting it from the tablet and handing it to Kassimir.

"Here's what I would like you to do. Get back with Gillespie and say you got a little interest. Strictly on a low key speculative basis. No mention that this really means anything..."

"I understand, sir," Garth replied, recognizing the order implicit in the words, as well as the urgency. "I'll call him... set up a visit. We got on pretty well." He got up and Kassimir pointed back through the living room. "Why don't you go into the library to make your call. Just turn right," Kassimir said, and Garth followed his directions.

"What do you think, Will?"

"I dona' know, Sam. What I do know is that Congress is in session, the court's sitting, and both the President and the Vice President are in town. And then there's the cabinet officers, the joint chiefs, with all their staffs."

"Exactly, we're talking about the people who make the American government operate. Civilians will be in the tens of thousands at least."

"Do we brief the White House?" Will asked, looking at Kassimir, and for a moment they just looked at one another and reckoned with what they were talking about. Then Will asked, "Thing is, how are we going to keep this a secret? I mean people who know are already freaked out that the device is in circulation in the world."

"You're right, Will. If this got out there could be a panic. Believe me, this is what's making my ample gut hurt. The entire city's going to come unglued if this gets out. But is it real? I mean, what do I say? What will I say to Bobbie at the White House: a psychic told me..."

"Whatever you're gonna say, Sam, I think you should arrange to say it as soon as you can, but not until this material has been checked out, and I think we should do that with the highest priority."

"I agree," Kassimir said, as Garth came back into the room.

"Michael Gillespie and I are meeting at the Hill Center, the foundation that funds him through the university. We're scheduled at one so I have to get going, sir. He's arranged for me to meet the viewers. He wants me to brief them; it's the only way he'll cooperate."

"You know what to say," Kassimir said, as a statement not a question.

"I think so, sir."

"Then good hunting, Jake."

"Thank you, sir," Garth said. He excused himself, went out, got into his car and drove back down the George Washington Parkway.

As he was doing so, at the Hill Center the viewers and staff, alerted by Michael's group text, were trickling in, packing into the center's classroom, the only space with enough chairs; some had even brought their partners. Weldon was the last to arrive, and he was left standing leaning against the wall.

When they were all settled Michael went to the front and began, "Jake Garth will be here anytime now. Before he gets here let me give you some background. He has something to do with the world where science and the military intersect. I've only met him once and that was through Barbara," Michael said, nodding in Barbara's direction "In fact, let's be honest, I met him because of Barbara. I don't think he would have taken the meeting if it had it just been me cold calling," he added, and everyone in the room looked at Barbara, who sat in her power wheelchair and waved the comment away.

"We spoke earlier today, and this may be the answer to the question we all want answered: What do ordinary people do when they know something like this?" Michael continued, "He tells me 'they', whoever they are, know nothing about any terrorist threat involving a nuclear bomb, and he was very upfront saying they don't know how to assess remote viewing data. The government funded some research back in the final decades of the twentieth century, but there is no one today who has had direct experience with the kind of thing we do. In other words, he's telling me in advance they don't know what to make of this." Around the room this provoked smiles and shrugs.

Then Michael's tone dropped and his expression became very serious. "I do not believe any of this. I see no reason why this data should be any different from our earlier research, and we know its accuracy rate. I believe our scenario is correct in its basic elements. Also I don't think he would take a meeting from a stranger on a Sunday afternoon unless there were something. So we are not being told the truth, as I see it." Around the room heads nodded in affirmation.

Just as Michael finished the doorbell rang, because Karen had locked the front door. She got up, went down the hall, opened the door, and came back with Garth.

Michael shook hands with Garth and turned to the group, "I don't think anyone here, besides Barbara and myself knows Jake Garth. Jake, this is the lab staff and the viewers we discussed," Michael said indicating each as he gave their name. "Jake, you know Barbara. This is Tracy Walsh, Weldon Shelcraft, Constance Walters. And this is John Sacks, Jefferson Yu and his wife Zhi Ruo, Istaqa Chester, and Raj

Chandra. As you can see we take this so seriously that some have brought their partners. I asked them to all come so that they would hear what you had to say directly from you."

Garth took in the room and saw a middle aged Black woman who looked like a teacher, a stocky Sikh in a turban, a pretty woman with tattoos, a man who looked like an Indian warrior out in the old West, and a very large, very physical looking Black man in workmen's clothes, and thought to himself, "Who are these people?" Some were not even citizens probably, he thought, they looked like immigrants. How, he wondered, had they blundered into the most tightly held secret in America? Garth found himself caught off guard. This was not at all what he had expected. He was irritated to be put on the spot like this, but tried to put a good face on it.

"I didn't expect all these people, and this isn't at all what I… I'm not here to make a speech. In fact, that's a good place to start. I don't want to make too much about any of this," he said to the room. "I've gone over the records of your sessions and heard something about remote viewing from Professor Gillespie, who has given us complete access to the material for each session. You have exhibited exemplary citizenship."

"However, I want to stress that nothing is being done on an emergency basis. Please don't misunderstand. Without meaning any offense… We are treating this seriously, the same way we would treat any tip… We check out everything very thoroughly; we would be derelict if we did otherwise anywhere. But this is also Washington, D.C., with all three branches of government, from the President to the most junior congressman in town right now. But again, I want to stress that nothing we know suggests the emergency you're describing."

"What do you think we should do?" Jefferson Yu asked Garth. "I mean...should we leave town... should we tell other people?"

Garth looked at Yu, saying, "Good questions. Let me answer them emphatically. You should tell no one. Good God... nothing could be more irresponsible than starting a rumor about something like this. I really must insist that you all keep this strictly to yourselves. As to what you should do... you should do whatever you planned to do before this got started. I know you all believe very strongly in your psychic work. But...I repeat... there is nothing to suggest that it is accurate in this case. We are just doing proper due diligence."

He gestured to Barbara, adding, "I came here as a courtesy to Professor Strickland, and because Professor Gillespie gave me his material and, as I said, because we check everything out. But I don't want to make an emergency out of this."

Weldon, who had been leaning against the wall, stood straight, saying, "Would you tell us if there was one...?"

"I think that is very unfair... We're going to examine everything you think will happen, and we'll report back to Professor Gillespie," Garth said, then stopped, taken aback by Barbara's and Michael's open mistrust. The others saw this, and the entire atmosphere in the room chilled.

"We've given you everything we have," Michael said, offended and wanting to bring things to a close. "But as you said, at least we did what a citizen should."

Garth understood he had made a mistake, but as he thought about it, given his instructions about confidentiality, there was no way out of it. So he just said, "Thanks. I can't think of anything else except to thank you for being good citizens... we appreciate it when people get involved. We'll check it all out... and I can assure you we are very thorough."

Garth shook Michael's hand and left. All the others stayed, and the mood in the room was tense and alarmed.

John Sacks voiced everyone's hope. "I guess we let the Feds do their stuff, eh?"

Constance, who had been quiet up to then, burst out with the core issue about which they were still all unclear. "Is it true? I think that's what we have to ask ourselves, and I think we agree it is. But what does that mean? That's what I can't work out. I mean, suppose whoever is planning to set that bomb off does it a day early... or before they catch them. I've been having trouble sleeping. Herbert's on duty or he would be here. We're asking ourselves if he should talk to his commander. But we're afraid of doing just what that man said, starting a rumor. It could get entirely out of hand. But then I ask myself, How do we know it's not a war?"

John picked up her mood and tone. "That's right. Everyone seems to talk about this as a bomb. How do we know it isn't many bombs?"

Michael responded, "I thought of that. The problem was, none of you could do further viewing. We're all so saturated with our fears and beliefs. I called friends in Seattle, San Francisco, and San Diego and asked them to view this same time, without saying why. They saw nothing unusual, but one of the viewers at the Brain-Mind Institute in La Jolla said he felt a sense of potential tragedy back East."

"Well... that's it, then," Sacks said. "We're locked into a future that can't be changed. We've already seen it. It has to happen."

"That's right," Constance replied. "That's what my husband said. If you believe any of this, you have to believe all of it."

Sacks got up, as did Jefferson Yu and his wife, a rather severe looking Chinese woman, who said, "We're leaving..."

Her husband interrupted, "...I'm sorry Michael, but Zhi Ruo and I are going to visit her brother in Raleigh." The couple started to move toward the door, then stopped and Yu turned back. "I gotta be honest with you. I think it's irresponsible not to act on information like this... when you have it. And I don't care what that guy Garth says. I'm going to recommend to my friends they get out of town as well."

Naomi Wilson, a very attractive paramedic in her early thirties, stood up as well. "Michael, you know my mother is bedbound. I have to get her out of town. I'm sorry"

"I understand, Naomi," Michael said.

Raj Chandra, very upset, stood up, looked at Michael and Tracy and said, "I've got to move my Bitcoin mining rig. I've got 12 GPUs working, and I'm part of a pool. This is a nightmare," he blurted out as he struggled into his jacket and started out of the room. "And the downtime. If I work nonstop I may be able to get my rig relocated the day before this is supposed to happen. Ohh… I can't believe this," he ended as he ran down the stairs.

John Sacks, who had come with his husband Jerry, said, "We're taking my sister and her kids. Jerry and I have decided we will give the staff a week's paid vacation, and tell them to leave, although we won't say why.

"I understand," Michael said. "How many kids does your sister have?"

"Four, ages 12, 10, 8, and 4. Her husband was a Marine; he was killed in Syria. That's why we have to go. If everything falls apart someone will have to be there to help," John said, and Jerry, a very handsome commercial model, nodded his agreement.

"We're going to leave in the morning. We're going down to our country place in the Virginia Blue Ridge Mountains." Then looking Michael in the eyes, he added, "For what it's worth, I don't think that federal guy, whatever agency he is with, is going to feel any obligation to keep you in the loop as to what is happening. You have Tracy and Barbara and Sarah to think of. And yes, I know you are together," John said, and in response to Michael's reaction, smiled and added, "I think it's very sweet. But I also think you ought to plan your own escape. Get tucked away from everything someplace." With that he and Jerry went out, closing the door.

As soon as they were gone, Weldon looked at Michael and asked, "Is it possible to change a future once it has been seen? Is that a possibility, Michael?"

"I'm not sure, Weldon," Michael said, looking at him, identifying with his emotion. "This is what I think, though, and I think Barbara agrees," he said, looking over at Barbara, who knew what was coming because they had spent hours discussing it. She looked at Weldon and nodded affirmatively.

Michael went on. "When you remote view the future, what you are reporting, if you are accurate, is the highest probability future seen from that moment. When we do targets, the probability is close to 100 percent that that future will, in fact, happen. You know the computer could malfunction. But basically it is on track. But something like this is nowhere near as fixed. There are all kinds of variables, most of which we don't even know, and their strength or weakness is not fixed, and they change the probabilities."

"So we could change this," Weldon said, looking with great intensity at Michael.

"Yes, I think so, but how is not so simple. That's what we need to think about."

"I get it. Well, I'm in," he said, looking around the room at Barbara and Tracy. "I'm going to go home now and make some arrangements. And I'm also going to tell some people they should get out of town. I don't care what the government says. There are some people I love, and that's what's going down." Weldon got up and hugged Barbara and Tracy, and left, saying, "Call me and tell me what you decide, and what I need to do."

Barbara took that cue, and said, "Me too," and wheeled herself over to the elevator and took it down.

Finally it was just Michael and Tracy, and they went upstairs to Michael's office.

"Michael, I'm really scared. I understand why everyone is doing what they are doing. Connie, for instance. I am sure she is thinking about all her kids, and what to do. I feel the same," she said, and went into his arms. "I don't know... I think I've got to at least get Sarah down to my mother's in Fredericksburg. The problem is Keith. He will never go along with it. Taking her out of school, out of the district. Oh, God, this is so crazy..."she said, and Michael held her closer and kissed her temple.

They stood there for a long moment, with Michael cradling Tracy's head against his shoulder.

"I wish I knew what to say. Absolutely.... if it will make you more comfortable, let's send Sarah away. Damn. We should send the whole school away."

"It's like we're trapped. It's a curse to see the future. I never understood that before."

CHAPTER TWENTY-THREE

24 November — Washington, D.C. —

Jefferson and Zhi Ruo Yu were very distraught as they drove home from the center. They felt as if they were slipping back in history to the stories their parents had told them about social violence in China.

"Husband, we can't just leave. What about the shop, what about the employees?" Zhi Ruo said as they drove up Wisconsin avenue to their Maryland suburb.

"I think we have to close the shop, and tell the employees to leave town as well," Jefferson answered her.

"Lǎogōng," she said, an endearment acknowledging that they would be together for a long time. "I agree."

Jefferson took a hand off the wheel and gently touched her arm, saying, "But it's more than the shop. I am unclear, I confess to you; I do not know what to do."

"Let us drive in silence, perhaps some music, and think about this, and talk when we get home.

"Yes," Jefferson said, and turned on Pandora to the Chinese station they both liked. They rode home cocooned in the music, each with their own thoughts.

When they got to their ranch style house in Bethesda, they drove into their garage went into the house, made tea, and sat at their kitchen table.

"This is very painful," Jefferson said, and Zhi Ruo nodded her agreement.

"What do you think we should do?" she asked.

"I think we must tell family. There are five in the shop; they must be told. It will all have to be done on trust; we cannot say what it is. Michael's right. It would cause a panic. And to be truthful, what if all this is just wrong?"

"Do you think it is?" Zhi Ruo asked.

"No, I don't; that's why it's so difficult. I can't get the images of the session out of my mind," Jefferson said, putting his hand to his head for a moment.

"Then we must act on that, don't you think?"

"I do, and thank you dear wife."

"Family and the shop it will be, and we'll pay the staff. A week I think. If nothing happens it won't matter; if something does we cannot say what things will be like. That's what my father told me. You could not predict what would happen. This remote viewing is just one tiny little piece."

"My family said the same. How much will it cost?"

"It will be expensive, there is no way around that. We will just close for the week, give out some reason. There may be no bonuses this year, though."

Jefferson got up, and cleared the teacups, his wife washed them up, and he dried them. A couple long married in a familiar task. It gave them comfort.

"We will arrange everything in the morning," Jefferson said as they turned out the lights and walked down the hall.

Like the Yus, Weldon got back to this apartment, went in and sat down. He lived alone. He had almost married once, but then he had gone into the army, and she was gone when he came back.

He never knew his father who had only come around a few times. He doubted he would recognize him if he saw him on the street. And after his mother was hit by a car and killed—they never caught the driver—he was raised by his grandmother, and mostly on his own.

Because of his size, people were either afraid of him or wanted him to get involved in something that required muscle and was illegal. His uncle, his mother's brother, had died in prison, and he had no intention of hanging with gangs and going that route. That meant he was mostly alone.

At 18, to get out of his neighborhood and the life he had grown up in, he joined the army. Two tours, one in Afghanistan the other in Syria, had left him greatly changed. He couldn't live with anyone. He became a house painter because he could work alone, even if there was a crew.

Strangely, remote viewing helped. The experience for him was something like getting stoned on marijuana. Your mind opened to things you hadn't even been aware of. Your senses opened, was the way he thought of it.

The people at the Center had changed his life. He loved Barbara, and found it hard to believe that a ghetto-raised Black kid would find anything in common with a middle-aged Louisiana White woman in a wheelchair, who also happened to be a world famous physicist, but he did. And so did she.

Michael and Tracy had also become very dear to him. He felt very protective of them and Barbara. He was surprised how much he enjoyed children, and showing them the wilderness in safe doses. Particularly, he liked Coyote. They were both loners, didn't talk all that much, but they liked rock climbing and hiking together. Growing up, except for when he went to rural Maryland to visit his uncle, who was a fireman, he never saw trees that weren't surrounded by concrete or asphalt. Had never seen a deer or a rabbit until he went into the service. Other than the friendships with the men and women with whom he had served, the one good thing he got from those years was a love for wild places, and the ability to be competent in them.

He dialed Coyote, who picked up on the third ring.

"What are you doing?" he asked.

"I've been thinking about that. What are you going to do?

"I'm going to do whatever Michael and Tracy need."

"You're not getting out of town."

"No. I don't know what they want, but I am going to stick with them."

"I'd like to do that too. What do you think?"

"I think we should climb this rock together."

"Believe it or not I have to go to work. They couldn't get anyone else on such short notice, and I have to tell them I'm taking a week off. Not going to be pleasant."

"Yeah, I can see that. I'm going to bed."

"You can sleep?" Coyote asked.

"Sleeping even though a bomb may go off at any minute is not unfamiliar to me. Good night. I'll talk to you tomorrow, mid-day as usual," Weldon said, and hung up.

CHAPTER TWENTY-FOUR

25 November — Washington, D.C. —

Jake Garth was up at six a.m; it was still dark. He was scheduled to go out with the FBI tactical team and had to get into the same protective vest he had worn in Afghanistan, only in blue. They rode out as a caravan of black SUVs until they got to the consensus zone Michael had given them. They parked the cars, and as Garth got out, he looked to his left and could just see the top of the Capitol and the House office buildings. It gave him chills. This was every intelligence agent's worst nightmare. The men quickly assembled; he gave them a final briefing and they began to move systematically through the neighborhood. Other staff, who weren't sworn agents so they didn't carry weapons, followed, photographing and videoing everything.

While the search team was going door-to-door, in the Homeland Security communications bus technicians were capturing every phone both hardwired and wireless, as well as every device on the internet. Drones fed back their imagery. In the search area everything was being monitored, everything recorded.

As they entered each building some of the agents went to locate the janitors and had them guide them into the garages and store rooms where, as the janitors looked on, they searched every trunk, every box. Other agents went up to front doors and knocked. If an adult opened they showed the picture of Farouk. If a child opened they asked them, then asked for their mommies or daddies. It was incredibly tedious work. The agents hated it, but did it anyway. They had been told terrorists might have hidden a bomb, no mention of its nuclear nature.

Midway through the day, thanks to somebody posting something on social media, the media showed up, and Garth found himself staring into a dozen microphones and cameras; he hated it. Thinking as quickly as he could he told them, "We had a tip of possible terrorist activity, and we are checking it out. That's what we do to keep the American public safe."

In answer to the shouted questions, he responded, "We have found nothing. I told you it was just a tip, but we acted on it." Then when a particularly persistent reporter kept challenging him, he said, "Don't you think this is what we ought to be doing, what the American people have a right to expect their government to do?"

That seemed to take most of the steam out of the questions, and after assuring the reporters once again that he had nothing of substance to report, he instructed the local police, who had arrived in the middle of his impromptu presser, to put up yellow tape to keep the media people out of the way. By then a crowd had gathered, and they too had to be held back.

The whole thing left Garth feeling frustrated and harassed. He had Sam Kassimir's voice in his head, could imagine what he would say, and was not surprised when Sam called him. But he was surprised to hear Sam say, "You handled it very well Jake. Just keep at it."

Finally, after about five hours, the senior agent came up to Garth, saying, "We've checked every house in five blocks.

Nothing. I don't think much of this anonymous tip, Jake. Do you know how many hours we've got in this?"

"If the guy's here, we've got to find him. If he left anything, or has hidden anything, we've got to find that. What can I tell you?"

"Level with me Jake. What's this all about?"

"I wish I knew. I'm just like you, following orders."

By five o'clock everything they could think to search had been searched. Everyone they saw had been shown the picture. It had turned up nothing. Even the media was bored and began to pack up their vans and disperse. Finally, Garth called a halt. The agents got back in their SUVs and the whole caravan went back to the Hoover Building and left their gear.

"I'll file my report and copy you, Jake," the senior agent told him, adding, "but you already know this was a wild goose chase."

"Thanks," Jake said, then went down to the garage and got into his car, realizing the day was far from over and feeling conflicted about what had happened. He drove over to the office Kassimir had set up and found Belmore, Waterman, and Potter gathered around the conference table eating Chinese food someone had gone out to get for them.

He looked around as everyone looked back at him, and began, "There were astonishing correlations. Not just the picture of Farouk and the little train drawings. There are dozens of details that check out. Gillespie's people were right about all sorts of things. Things they just couldn't know… but somehow did. But no bomb, no sign of terrorists. We went to the lat-longs they gave us. I had the circled area, and I could tell you how many cockroaches there are in some of those buildings. That's how intense it's been. But the bottom line is...zip. Nothing."

Kassimir gestured for him to sit down, and when he did he told Garth once again, "Jake you handled yourself very well, no complaints from me." Then turning to the table he said, "Gentlemen. Now's the time for your thoughts."

Potter was not hesitant to respond. He had spent a lot of time thinking about what they were doing and had developed a clear opinion. "I think we're wasting our time. In fact... I'll go further. We know that bomb is out there, and we've been going on a mad psychic witch hunt when we should have been focusing on real intelligence."

Waterman picked up his thought, "I agree. If it's a vote you're after, Sam... I say drop it."

Kassimir pursed his lips and looked down for a moment, thinking. Then he looked up.

"Call it off, Jake. We're packing it in."

"Gillespie, et al...?"

"Yeah. But be nice. They were sincere. Set up a meeting some place anonymous so the media don't see you. Tell him to his face."

Garth left Kassimir and on the way home called Michael.

"Could we meet tomorrow? I have something to tell you. Not on the phone."

"Of course. Where?" Michael responded.

"Some place out to the way. How about the conservancy at the National Botanical Gardens?"

"That seems very mysterious, Jake, but Okay. What time?"

"Say ten hundred."

Michael was the first to arrive, and he was enchanted as he entered the conservancy; he hadn't been there in years. It was a miniature world of trees, plants, and birds, all beneath a conservatory of glass and iron. The overlapping calls of the birds provided a kind of background music, and some brightly colored exotic bird he couldn't identify flew past him overhead. He saw a bench and went over, sat on it, and allowed himself to just take it all in.

He realized how tense he was, and how much he needed this break. He thought about Garth, whom he had originally liked but about whom now he was very conflicted. He was sure Garth had lied to him at the meeting in the lab. He was so lost in these thoughts he didn't hear Garth until he came up and said, "Thanks for coming, Michael."

Michael got up; they shook hands and sat on the bench. Michael felt like he was in a spy movie. Before he could say anything Garth began speaking.

"It doesn't check out. Oh, lots of details were uncannily accurate.... but I gather that's not unusual. Your main point though, the location of the bomb, was wrong. There is nothing in the area you and Barbara selected that supports the stories of your psychics."

"Have you... ?"

"... The answer is, yes. We've done everything that an unlimited government budget would suggest we might do; you probably saw it on the news," Garth said, shaking his head remembering it. "Hell, I know more about some of the buildings in that area then I do about my own house, and I've lived in it for 20 years."

"Don't call us, we'll call you...right?" Michael said, understanding he was being brushed off and wanting to get it over with.

"Candidly...yeah. But listen. I want to be clear about this. If I'd been in your shoes, I would have done the same thing. You were a good citizen. You did what good citizens are supposed to do. Nobody can fault you for that." With that Garth got up from the bench. "Wait five minutes before you leave," he said, and walked out.

Michael was happy to wait, allowed himself to sink back into the world of the conservatory, and ended up waiting thirty minutes as he thought about what to do next. He got up feeling confused and let down, and returned to the Hill Center where he found the viewers and staff who had not already left the area gathered in the conference room. He told them what had happened, and felt their confusion, their loss of hope, and their anger.

"Basically, it was, don't call us. Good citizenship award...but don't call. I don't know. You can't blame them. I want to go around the room. I need to know. What sense of the truth of all this do each of you have?"

"I think it's real. I've thought it was real from the beginning. I don't know what to do...No!, I know one thing... I'm going to get Sarah out of the city," Tracy said with great passion in her voice.

"I'll do what ever you say, Boss. But I told my grandmother to go visit her sister in Atlanta," Wheldon said, and he and Michael traded a look.

"Thank you. There's nothing to do right now," Michael said.

Coyote and Weldon, sensing that Tracy and Michael needed to talk, got up and excused themselves, saying they would check in later.

"I've reached my limit," Wildredo Sanchez spoke up. "I know what I'm going to do; I'm taking leave and going to Florida for a week," he said, and got up and left.

Barbara wheeled her chair closer to where Michael and Tracy stood, and said, "We need to talk."

"I'm sorry Barbara, it will have to wait. The person I need to talk to is Keith," Tracy said, and she walked down the hall telling Siri to call Keith.

"It's you and me, kid," Barbara said, looking up at Michael. "Let's have a mohita. I still have some mint in the greenhouse," and she wheeled over to the elevator.

"I'll meet you there," Michael responded, going out into the hall and down the stairs.

A few minutes later Tracy found them in Barbara's small conservatory at the back of the house. "Keith and I are going to have dinner at Martin's," Tracy said, adding, "I wanted to do this in a public place." She turned and walked back down the hall and out onto the sidewalk, turned right and began walking down the herringbone brick sidewalk to Wisconsin Avenue, where the venerable Martin's pub was to be found.

She got there just as Keith did. He had taken an apartment on N Street, even though it was hard on their salaries for each of them on their own to rent in Georgetown. But they both wanted Keith to be within walking distance, and on balance, Tracy was glad they had been able to work it out.

The meal started civilly enough. There had been a time when they had been comfortable together, and they fell back on those remembered rituals, almost getting through the meal when Tracy said, "You know, I was thinking, Keith. Maybe it would be a good idea to send Sarah down to my mother's for a few days. They haven't seen each other in months, and you know how much she loves her grandmother.

"No."

"What kind of an answer is, 'No.'?"

"It would be hard to make it simpler. I don't know what you're up to Tracy, but I will not permit Sarah..."

"Permit...permit!" Tracy said, her voice rising, as nearby diners turned to look. "Listen to you," She went on more quietly, "You sound like some pompous politician. Where do you get off with this 'permit' crap?"

"Listen to yourself, Tracy. You're hysterical. People are looking at us. How much more do you need to convince yourself you're coming apart? Talk it over with Dr. Goldman. See what she says. You need some help."

"Please, Keith," Tracy said trying another tack. "It would just be for a few days. Please do this for me. Whatever you think about me... please do this."

"No. Sarah's not going anywhere, and certainly not out of the District. I'm sorry. If I have to I will get an injunction... I'm not getting into a custody battle where I have to extradite my own child from another state. I've got to go," Keith said, standing, reaching into his pocket and throwing money on the table. "Do yourself a favor. Talk to Dr. Goldman. I meant what I said," he went on, his face contorted in anger, but his voice steely and calm.

CHAPTER TWENTY-FIVE

27 November — Warrenton, Virginia —

In the predawn darkness Farouk, now without his beard and wearing a hair piece, with half glasses around his neck, was sitting on an upturned box in a rundown hangar in rural Maryland. The doors were open part way, and he was staring up at the sky. Next to him, on another carton, was a young earnest looking man in his twenties.

"In the desert... outside of Alexandria... when I was an engineering student...the night before the '73 war... I was nineteen. I sat just like this in a hangar. They were going to drop us in Israel. We were a team of four. Our job was to destroy a phone switching complex. I was so full of doubts and fears..."

"I have no fears like that. I remember my eight-year-old sister Fatima as I saw her after the American planes strafed our camp. There were no doubts after that," the younger man replied.

"Are you sure, Said? I would not force you, even if I could."

"You mean about dying? How can a man fear dying when it is God's will? My family are gone. There is no one. When my mother was killed by the Israelis I swore I would have my revenge. Is it not right for a man to avenge his family?"

"It is your right," Farouk said, touching the younger man on his arm. "And your duty... it is a holy cause."

A truck pulled up and two men came out of the darkness and walked into the hangar. Both were brawny White men dressed in camo, with bellies. One had the lightning SS symbol tattooed on one bicep and the number 88 on the other. The other man was somewhat older. Each carried one end of a metal case. Both spoke with American accents. The older one leaned down to Farouk

"Here it is," he said, and set the case down in front of Farouk.

"Thank you, and thank your people. The money has been transferred," Farouk said, holding up his phone.

"We know, we checked before we drove in," the young man with the tattoos said. It was clear from his tone and expression that he did not like Farouk or Said. "What's in this by the way?"

"The explosives that we will use."

"I could've gotten you all the dynamite you needed," the younger man bragged. "I don't know what all this is about, but I won't kid you, I don't like Muslims."

"I don't like you either," Farouk said, not taking offense. "But it is in all our interests to make this happen."

"He's right, you fucktard," the older White man said to the younger. "And we have the commander's orders, Darrell, so let's not get up in anybody's face. Okay?"

"I don't like you, Darrell, but that isn't the point," Farouk continued, trying out the name. "Your friend is right. We are all working to do this. It has taken more than you know to get this set up."

"When do you want us back?" The older man asked.

"I'll need you here just before noon tomorrow, say 11:45, and you'll stay until Said takes off. Make sure all the arrangements are in place for Moustapha and myself."

The men nodded and left the hangar, got into a van and drove away.

"Christians," Moustapha spat out. "Heathens. They make me feel unclean. Particularly the young one; he hates us, Farouk. Are you sure the bomb has not been tampered with?"

"Look here," Farouk said, showing that the wire and lead seal had not been tampered with. "It hasn't been opened. Help me get it over to the plane." The two men picked up the case and carried it over to the side of the plane.

"You're right, he does hate us, but they drove it up from Virginia. This was set up well above their level. They have no idea what we have planned. They think it is some kind of conventional explosive. He may hate us but he likes what we are doing. He thinks it will end with his group taking over America," Farouk said.

"Will it?" Moustapha asked.

"I don't think so. The general thinking, and I agree with it, is that it will tear America into factions even worse than today, and break the union up, or render it so disabled that they will not be able to keep pressure on what we want to do in the righteous world of Allah, blessed be his name. I think it will end the decades of war in our lands."

"That sounds fine to me," Moustapha said, and went back into the hangar office.

Farouk and Said returned to sitting as before, looking out of the hangar as the sky grew lighter.

Farouk gently put his hand on Said's shoulder.

"Is there anything I can get for you? Do you want to make your video?"

"Pray with me. Join me at first prayers. Pray that I may be a perfect messenger."

All three men went into an office where there was a heater and a shabby carpet. One by one they went into the bathroom and did the ritual cleansings, then picked up the carpet and carried it out to the front of the hangar, where as the sun was rising they knelt down and did the morning Fajr prayer.

Afterwards they took the carpet back and set up a video camera and two lights, and Said Masdi made his last statement.

CHAPTER TWENTY-SIX

27 November — Washington, D.C. —

The early morning found Michael already at the lab going over the session records one more time. He felt incredibly harried, and like the rest of them he really wasn't sure what to do. One option was to assume Jake Garth was right; there was nothing there, and write the experience off.

The other was to trust in the accuracy percentages from past work, and his gut told him that's what he should do. But he realized it was one thing to make a call on an abstract lab experiment like describing a photograph, or even something more concrete like an archaeological site, and another to accept that unless he could find a way to change the probabilities a nuclear bomb was going to explode in Washington in approximately fifty-six hours, just as the viewers had described. He found it very hard to calculate the reality of that. At about eleven Weldon came in, and Michael could tell something had provoked him

"Weldon... what's going on man? You're drunk."

"Yeah. I am. Fired. Got fired. Job was gonna take a week. I thought...what the hell? What's the point? Went out for lunch. Thought, what the hell's the point. Told them I couldn't start for a week. They said they couldn't wait," Weldon said in an angry bitter tone.

"I'm sorry, Weldon," Michael said, now fully engaged in the emotion of his friend.

"Don't worry about it. What's the point?"

"You want to crash on the couch in my office, or go over to my house?"

"Nah. Thanks."

"You can't drive."

"You're right. Wouldn't want to break any rules just as the world is blowing up," Weldon said in a more sober but even more unhappy voice. "Don't worry, I called Uber; they'll take me home. They got me here," he added. "I came to tell you that if you and Barbara are staying, I'm staying. If you're leaving I'm leaving. If you need me let me know. Coyote feels the same. We talked yesterday; we'll do whatever you need. I assume you have in mind to stop this, so you can count me and Coyote as a team," Weldon said sort of belligerently. Then his phone rang and the Uber car was there.

As Weldon left, the phone rang. Michael picked it up.

"Michael Gillespie.... Hello, Dean Hopple. How are you. Yes.... fine ... Dr. Goldman? We've met. I wouldn't say we know one another. No connection with my research at all... why do you ask?... the ethics committee... I see. I'll get it in writing.... The Hill Trust as well... I see. Lee, it's... no I understand. I wouldn't put you in that position. Of course, I'll respond immediately... as soon as I receive it. About a week, you say," Michael said with a laugh that was not pleasant. "No, I don't think it's funny either." He hung up the phone understanding his entire career now hung mostly on the good will of his dean. He shrugged; compared to a nuclear explosion, how should he regard it? He looked at the phone and turned back to his work.

Downstairs Barbara, alone in her apartment, sat in front of her computer. She turned and wheeled herself over to her coffee maker, poured a cup of coffee and looked out through the French doors of her conservatory to the garden beyond. In the background Pandora's Café Del Mar station was just changing albums. She sat quietly in her chair, listening to *Stars* by Helen Jane Long. When she finished her cup she put it in the sink and pushed herself back to her workstation. Like Michael she did not know what to do. Should she leave? Michael clearly was not going to leave, and neither was Tracy, she believed. Coyote and Weldon would do what was asked of them. What should she do?

She sat staring out at the garden, and thought about her life and saw again that it was her grit and intellect that got her through. She was a girl from Breaux Bridge on Bayou Teche in Louisiana. She had been a gawky stick with bright red hair from a Scottish merchant mariner grandfather.

Things changed when she was thirteen, and in her mind she could see her teenage self. She began developing a figure that made boys from her school, and their dads as well, turn to look, but not get too close, because when roused she had a withering wit that made people laugh, but also humiliated.

Her grades and gift for math—she was past her math teacher by the tenth grade—were what got her out of Breaux Bridge. She got a statewide scholarship to LSU, and discovered science.

It was a coincidence that she now saw as a synchronicity. Her boyfriend at the time, and as she thought of him he came back into her mind; she could see his black curls and for just a moment feel his body in hers. He wanted to be an engineer and had to take a science course, and he chose physics. So she did as well, and fell in love.

That led her to MIT for her masters and doctorate. She thought of those years as the time it took to master the tools, the mathematics, the laws, how to do the papers, even the way to speak to people. By the time she had done that, physics had become a kind of music for her. Not of sound but of harmonies.

At forty-five she won the Nobel. The trip to Stockholm, and her feelings just before she stepped up to the podium in the city's historic Concert Hall to give her address were sacred memories.

The other memory in this chain was very different. It was the summer evening as she lay on a dock looking up at the stars, having smoked a particularly good number, that she had the insight into the nature of information which won her the prize. It had taken her almost a year to translate that experience into the equation that won her the prize. Everything was wonderful, until the following year when her car was t-boned by a drunk driver who killed himself and left her in a wheelchair.

In the emergency room where she was taken she had had a near death experience. It confirmed for her the existence of nonlocal consciousness, consciousness that was not physiologically dependent, and the central role of information. She did not talk about her NDE; she only told her doctor, on the condition of anonymity, so that he could use her experience and the neurological data in a multiple institution study.

At nearly forty-eight she came out of the experience with the path of her life changed, and a celibate, something she could never have imagined for herself. She had sustained severe nerve damage and had no sensations in her pelvis at all. It had not been easy to admit to herself that she was a woman in a wheelchair who would never again experience an orgasm. But accepting that, she decided, did not mean she could not once again be vivacious and stylish. She could have a good time, and she could still love.

It took over a year and multiple surgeries to get her to a place where she could think without discomfort somewhere in her body nagging her. But finally it passed, and she went back to work.

She retained her endowed chair at MIT and, at first, continued the same line of research, but soon left that. In the many hours she had lain in bed, pain or no pain, she became increasingly focused on the relationship of consciousness and information, beyond quantum, which was where Planck, the father of QM, had been headed, she was now convinced.

Barbara had been a dedicated materialist. But during that year of rebuilding her body, when she thought about that night on the dock, she now saw it as an earlier example of opening to nonlocal consciousness. In the final months of her rehabilitation she had begun to think about insight and to wonder how it had occurred to other people like her, individuals who had had insights that changed the game. She could see that insight was another way of opening to nonlocal consciousness.

At meetings, if they seemed open to it, she talked to fellow laureates. She read, and saw that countless men and women who had had those kind of insights that changed the world were much like her. French mathematician Henri Poincaré had one of his as he crossed the street. Mozart spoke of hearing the music as he rode in a carriage or lay in bed, and then writing it down. Brahms said something very similar. Tesla's vision of the electric motor as he walked across Central Park was another account she came across. It seemed obvious to her that there was a recurring theme: information and consciousness.

As she delved ever deeper into her research she became increasingly convinced that consciousness had to be part of physics if civilization was going to survive. It left her with a sense of obligation and she agreed to serve on foundation boards and research committees where she smiled and leaned in support of postmaterialist science. She came to understand that that had been her motive in not talking about her NDE. She did not have to defend against charges of bias.

One of the boards she had gone on was the Hill Foundation. She had accepted the appointment because they had a record of funding both environmental and consciousness-oriented research. Knowing her interest, the Research Director had sent her a grant application Michael had written. It immediately spoke to her, because through remote viewing he was dealing with nonlocally sourced information that could be objectively verified. From the proposal it was obvious to her that Michael had reached the same conclusions she had, and had operationalized what she had theorized. Like herself he understood that the big question was: what is information?

She arranged for him to come to Cambridge and took him to lunch. They liked each other immediately. Her math skills, her command of physics were far past his. But he had an operational command of the processes of consciousness that she could not equal, had never even considered.

She had never told him, but she had asked the Hill family to fund Michael's center and to build her apartment there. Ostensibly it was because the National Science Foundation wanted her to be nearby, which they did, and enthusiastically supported the Hills. In fact it was because she wanted to work with Michael. She felt that between them they might make a real breakthrough, and she could see Tracy playing a role as well.

Her chiming clock brought her out of her reverie leaving her sure about what she was going to do. If Michael, as she suspected he would, decided to try and stop the bomb, she would join him.

She wheeled herself back into her office and began to go over the data again. Her decision had left her relaxed, as she called the screens up.

Upstairs, after he thought Sarah would be asleep, Michael called Tracy. She burst into tears on the phone and he told her, "I'll come over."

When he arrived she was calmer but he could see the strain in her face and her posture.

"Keith won't cooperate," she said in her hallway before turning to lead him into the living room. They sat on the couch, and Tracy curled her body into Michael's as he put his arm around her.

"I don't know what to do, Michael. I can't tell him why. If I did he would just think it was further proof I was mentally deranged and tell me to see Dr. Goldman."

"Lee Hopple called me today. Goldman has filed a formal ethics violation against me. The Hill Trust has been notified. Even if the charge is dismissed I could lose my funding, I'm sure."

"Oh, my God. Over what?"

"When you were in the hospital... a million years ago it seems now, Goldman told me that if I did not stop involving you in the research she would file charges. I never told you....

I never really took her seriously, I guess," he said, shaking his head.

"Michael,.. what is happening? What are we going to do? Everything is going crazy."

"I don't know. I don't know. When you know something like this, and you tell your government about it, and they say there is nothing there, what do you do?... it's like getting hit by a train," Michael said. "I'll be honest, I am torn; maybe Connie and Sacks and the rest are right. Maybe we ought to bag this and just get out of town. If we're wrong, who cares? If we're right, we're alive. But then I think of a million dead people, and you just can't walk away from that."

"Then neither can I," Tracy said and kissed him.

They both heard a noise and looked over to see Sarah standing in the doorway.

"I had a bad dream, Mommy."

"Oh, sweetheart... here, let's go back to check that no monsters are in your room," Tracy said as she got up and crossed to where her daughter stood, taking her hand.

"No... Michael. He checks better than you, Mommy."

"Right you are," Michael said, and got up. "Come on then. Monsters beware..."

Michael and Sarah went down the hall to her bedroom. While Tracy was waiting the telephone rang.

"Hi. Barb.... Lousy, to be honest. He's on monster patrol... Sarah had a bad dream... I've just been informed that he's a superior checker. Yeah. I'll have him call you.... Wait, I think he's coming."

Michael re-entered the room, and Tracy handed him the phone.

"It's Barb. Something's up."

Michael looked at her quizzically. "Yeah, Barb... You're kidding.... I'll be right over. Yeah. Gimme five minutes."

Michael hung up the phone and frantically began putting on his shoes, almost falling in the process.

"What's happened?"

"Barb's found a mistake. Something that affects everything. I'll call you as soon as I know," Michael said, pulling on his jacket, stooping to kiss Tracy, then running out of the room.

He jogged the blocks to the Hill Center and down the ramp to Barbara's basement flat, went in and knocked on her door and heard her say, "It's open."

He went in and found Barbara at her worktable. She turned and beckoned him over.

"I was mistaken. The blast does not come from within a building but above it. I assumed it was in a building close to the rooftop. That's what Jake and his people also assumed. That's the M.O. for terrorists. But what if it were a light plane? The investigators found nothing in any of the buildings because there was nothing to find. The bomb's point of detonation was above them, but only a few hundred feet. It was just random that the plane was there at all. I think they were on their way somewhere else, and something went wrong."

Michael pulled a chair over and sat down next to Barbara, and she handed him the keyboard. He called up the session data and they went through it together. In the midst of this Michael's phone rang, it was Tracy. She told him one of her regular babysitters, a college student in the building, could babysit Sarah, and she was coming over.

"Yes, come over," he said. "I think we've got it." He disconnected and turned to Barbara. "Tracy asked one of the young women sharing an apartment in her building to baby-sit. She'll be over in a moment.," he said as they went back to work. They were deep into studying the material when there was a knock at the door, and Tracy came in.

Michael and Tracy embraced, and Barbara watched them and approved. Then she called to them and they went over, standing next to her, looking at the multiple screens on her worktable.

"The blast figures are perfect," she said. "In fact they're better than my original calculations."

"Barb believes the blast will come from a small light plane flying at a low altitude, probably to avoid radar," Michael explained in answer to Tracy's quizzical look. "The relationship to the building was purely random. That's where we all made the mistake. We thought it was near the rooftop. Barb now thinks it's a few hundred feet above it," Michael explained to her.

"It's hard to be precise with nuclear bombs, the force is so great," Barbara added.

"Are you going to call Garth?" Tracy asked.

"I don't know what I would say."

"You're right. The basic premise would still be questioned," Tracy said. "He'd just think we were trying to prove our outrageous theory."

"Don't bother with Jake. I talked to him yesterday. Very polite but just as you said... don't call us," Barbara concurred.

"We're going to have to get something more to make any of this believable," Michael said, looking at both women. "In fact to get their attention I think it is going to take calling them up and telling them something like 'come to 123 Main Street

I can see the bomb," he said shaking his head. "You realize what that means?"

"It means we're staying. The three of us?"

"No Coyote and Weldon want to come along."

"We're going to stop a nuclear bomb going off?" Tracy asked. "It sounds like a television show, Michael."

"Do you have an alternative?"

"No, but it still sounds like a television plot."

"Wait a minute," Barbara said. "This has been bugging me for days. There were some numbers, an odd string of numbers with a letter. We dismissed them as analytical overlay or…" she looked at Michael, "You thought it was a ham…"

"Yeah, but it didn't check out," Michael answered.

"We're down to hours. I think you should call Weldon and Coyote and ask them to come in."

"You're right.," Michael answered.

"I'll call them right now," Tracy said, pulling out her iPhone.

Then she stopped. "Those numbers. Could they be the ID number of a plane, or part of it?"

"A plane?" Michael asked

"The tail numbers," Tracy replied. " All planes have tail numbers. My cousin has a plane. I don't know what kind but it has one engine. I thought of it when you were telling me the bomb went off in the air. His plane has numbers like that on its tail."

"Bingo!" Michael said.

"Yes," Barbara agreed.

"Weldon. It's Tracy. Yeah… a little after two. We're on to something. Can you come over to Barbara's right away…. No, I mean right away. Now. Do you know where Coyote is?

He's with you, both of you come." To the others, "They'll be here. There won't be much traffic, it shouldn't take long." Then back into the phone, " Thanks Weldon... see ya."

When she hung up Michael said, "Let's take this to the conference room; the screens are bigger." When they were all together again, Barbara said, "As I was riding up the elevator I located the number in the database on my tablet "Here it is," she said, bringing N789 up on the room's big screens.

"Let's suppose it is part of a plane number, as Tracy suggests. We can check that, although it may not tell us where the plane actually is."

"You mean it's a rental," Tracy said.

"Yes, that's what I thought," Barbara replied. If I were going to set off a bomb I would rent a plane not buy one. If it is a small plane, as it would have to be, the rental wouldn't be too far away. If we're lucky we might find out which airport."

"I think you're right Barb. If I were doing this, I would have rented it somewhere close and flown it up here for a few days."

"If that's true the number may not be much help," Michael said.

"Not necessarily, Michael; the plane would have to land somewhere. They would certainly write down its number. I think the thing to consider are airports," Barbara said..

"I agree, Barbara," Tracy added.

"How would you get it in over the city without blowing off who knows how many security alarms? Jets scrambling... that sort of thing?" Tracy asked.

"Remember that psycho who got a helicopter as far as the White House lawn in the 70s... during the Nixon Administration," Michael responded.

"If you came in low, below radar... just a few hundred feet once you were in the city, coming from not too far away... moving as fast as you could. I think you could do it... particularly if you didn't plan to get back out. After all, it's a nuclear bomb; you don't have to be very precise," Barbara said, writing her calculations on her tablet for them to see.

"Of course!" Michael concurred.

"You've got to figure that anyone who could get hold of a nuclear warhead and get it all the way here, could surely find some fanatic pilot willing to die to explode it," Tracy added.

Barbara had picked up a tablet, and logged it on. "After looking at those maps and calculating probable speeds, I think we have it. It takes time to scramble jets, and they are not as close in." She paused, thought for a moment, then began again. "Even to get an armed helo aloft. So you would want to be as close-in as possible so you would be at your target before they could get to you."

"General aviation fields," Michael said, continuing Barbara's thinking. "Dulles, Friendship, or National would have too much security. Too much action. Too many places for things to go wrong. I need to think about this for a minute, and I need to go to the head."

Michael went off the bathroom, and while he was gone Barbara rolled her chair over to where Tracy was sitting.

"Tracy... I'm not sure you should get into this. You've got Sarah to think about."

"It's tearing me apart, Barbara. Keith threatened to get an injunction. He thinks it's all a trick to get Sarah out of state so that... I don't know what... so I can keep him from seeing her, I guess. It's so nuts. But, I'll bet he's done it... been to court. He's an engineer. He never leaves anything to chance.

What am I going to do? And Goldie has charged Michael with an ethics violation for allowing unstable me to participate in his experiments."

"You're serious," Barbara said, her face twisted in surprised alarm.

"Very. His Dean called him," she said as Michael was returning.

"Let's not get into that," Michael said. "That's for another day. I've was thinking about this general aviation idea. Barb, you see the wind coming from one direction. And we have to assume these people have figured they have a very limited time in the air before they are discovered. I think that limits where they can start from."

"You're right. Let me work it out," Barbara said, and began. They waited in silence for a moment and then she said, "All of these airfields must be East in Maryland or south in Virginia.

"How many airfields is that?" Tracy asked, and as she did so the doorbell rang. First Weldon's face and then Coyote's appeared in a window that popped up on one of the screens.

"While you're doing that," she said to Barbara and Michael, "I'll go down," and left the room.

"Don't tell them anything; I have an idea," Michael said.

Tracy opened the door for Weldon and Coyote, and gave each a hug when they came in. When they started to ask questions, she responded, "Just hold it for a minute. Michael has something in mind." They went up to the conference room, and as soon as they entered Michael called out, "Thanks for coming guys. I want to try something. Are you up for a session?"

"Sure."

"Weldon let's start with you, let's go to the egg." Looking at Barbara, Tracy, and Coyote he said, "Can you all wait half an hour? Then you Coyote. You two, not a word about what we have been discussing."

"Of course," Barbara answered, and the two men left.

When Weldon and Michael were in the egg and their bio monitors were in place, Michael logged the session in, then said to Weldon, " It is the 28ᵗʰ of November. You are in the place where the bomb is located. You are life size, all your senses report. I will say, target, and when I do please tell me what you perceive." After a beat, "Target."

"Dark."

"Are you inside or outside...?"

"Some kind of large structure. Hollow sounds.. metal maybe..."

"Are there people present?"

"Yes, several."

"Can you describe the sense impressions that come to you about what they are thinking and doing?

"There's one man in charge. He's a little older. They're getting ready to put the bomb in the plane. It involves something sticky. There's a something that looks like a gun, but it's not a gun."

"Go forward in time until they are actually putting the bomb in the plane. What sense impressions do you get?

"The bomb is going inside the plane. I see a recurring shape... metal... framework. They are joined together in some way. Here I will draw them for you," he said, and drew as sequence of shapes like an angular rib cage.

"That's it. That's what I get."

Michael, pressed the tablet and ended the session.

" Can you go up and ask Coytoe to come down?"

"Sure," Weldon said, taking off the bio-helmet. He got up and left. Michael stayed where he was staring at the drawing Weldon had made, then cleared the tablet for the next session.

A few minutes later, Coyote came into the egg, settled himself, and once again Michael logged in the session and stated the nonlocal task.

"I'm inside It's cold... not as cold as outdoors, but cold. The plane is there. Let me debrief analytical overlay and say this is a hangar. It's not slick and modern. It's almost like a garage but bigger. There's rust... I can smell petroleum."

"Are people present?"

"Yes. Several; there are two older men and a younger man. There are some other people involved, but they're not there at the moment. It's funny; they really don't like each other, but they're working together."

"Where is the bomb?"

"It's in a crate. They're going to put it in the plane. Only one of these people knows how to do this, the oldest man. He has fake hair on his head by the way."

"All right. I want you to go forward in time to when they are putting the bomb in the plane. What do you see?

"They're going to take it out of the crate. It's going to be, like stuck to metal..." Coyote paused and closed his eyes for a moment. " A little metal box... wiring insight of it... a small card shape... green... has metal in shapes on it. The box is gray."

Coyote closed his eyes again, and his body turned as if he were seeing something. He opened his eyes, "They're taking the plane apart... not completely, but something is being removed. It has a smooth surface... not very thick. Also a kind of a gray. They stick it to the plane, somehow. Something that comes out of a tube. I'll debrief glue."

"Debrief noted."

"I want to stop, Michael. I have a question," Coyote said.

"What is it?"

"It's the same question Weldon asked you. Is this all locked in? There used to be a Presbyterian preacher who came to my high school. He had a word for it… predestination. Is this predestined?"

"I don't think so. I think you and Weldon and the other viewers, as I said, are reading probabilities. Right now this is the strongest, most likely probability, the most numinous information architecture. But it's not one hundred percent. There are other ways the information architecture could be arranged. A lot can happen between the first viewing we did where you all saw the explosion, and what you have just described."

"Then let's do it. Let's stop this thing."

"I agree, and we have a plan. Let's go back upstairs," Michael said, and logged out of the session.

CHAPTER TWENTY-SEVEN

28 November — Washington, D.C.

Michael was hunched over his computer with Google Earth on all three screens showing the area of the five general aviation airfields they had found. It was five-thirty in the morning. He had slept on his fold-out couch and awakened after just a few hours, his head filled with questions.

He looked at the time and got up, quickly showered and dressed in clothes he kept for when he slept over as occasionally happened and went down the stairs to Barbara's apartment.

"It's open," he heard Barbara say when he knocked. He went in to find Barbara in her chair in the kitchen and Weldon overflowing both ends of her couch.

"It was crazy for him to drive home," she answered the question he hadn't asked. Their talking woke Weldon who sat up. He had only briefs and T-shirt on, and his muscularity was very much in evidence.

"He is very pretty, isn't he," Barbara said in a soft voice to Michael, who just laughed.

Weldon, who had heard her, just shook his head and went into the bathroom.

"Did you get any sleep?" Michael asked.

"Three hours, then I woke up with all this in my head," Barbara responded.

"Me too. I woke up thinking about what we worked out last night, and how we can do this. There are five airports within 100 miles. If we split up into three teams, Weldon in one car, Coyote in another, Tracy and I in the third car, and you down near Broad Creek, Maryland, I think we can just get every one of the airfields covered."

"Why not four cars, and why should I be in Maryland?" Barbara asked.

"Because Tracy is absolutely committed to getting Sarah out of town and I don't want her to have to do that alone. She's made some arrangement to have Sarah driven to her mother's."

Barbara's expression showed her support. "I'd be the same way.... But what about the injunction?"

"She's willing to take whatever penalty comes...if we're right...who cares about the penalty?"

"Why down in Broad Creek, Maryland?"

Michael looked seriously at Barbara and made strong eye contact, "Because it's outside of the danger circle you drew on the map last night. It's near two of the airports. You remember La Salle Du Bois, Andrés restaurant out in the country there.

"Of course, is that what you have in mind… no one ever forget's André or his restaurant."

"He's only open for dinner," Michael explained, "and when I called him he said we can use his office as a central exchange. Also, all of these airports are in rural areas, cellphone coverage can be very spotty. So, if we can we text each other, but we also each of us calls in every hour to you, even if we have to go to a landline and report what we find, and you can set up a Zoom conference call if we all need to be linked, or just send out a digest message."

Barbara looked at him intently, and after a silence he added, "If it all goes bad you'll be safe. You're important to a lot of people in ways none of the rest of us are, Barb. That's just the truth. Also, you'll be able to tell the story and because you're Barbara Strickland people will listen."

Tears ran down Barbara's cheeks as she looked at him, but her face did not break. "Oh, Michael," she reached out her hand and touched his arm. "I can't tell you... I will never forget that." Her body shivered, and she said, "We just need to make this work." She turned her chair slightly to indicate they were back to business.

"Michael, have you thought what you are going to do if you find this plane? It's a little late in life to become special ops," Barbara said, putting her hand on his arm.

"I don't know, yet... but I think what we talked about is the way to go. Once we have reason to believe we have found the airport we call in the cavalry." Michael tapped on his tablet. "Here's a copy of everything Weldon and Coyote will need," he said, passing the file on to her tablet. "The field locations, the drawing of the man. The plane numbers. Here's the directions for you," he said, passing on another file. "Andre expects you, as I said. If you and Weldon leave by eight o'clock everything should work. Tracy and I will check in at nine, and every hour thereafter. Coyote is going to the field near Winchester, Virginia."

"Okay, I have it, Barbara answered, as Weldon came out having showered and dressed. Michael explained what was needed, then went back to his office, called Tracy, and explained everything to her.

Like everyone else Tracy hadn't slept well, and she was very nervous. She had arranged with Caroline, one of the young women in the shared apartment, who was twenty-three and a nurse at Georgetown Hospital, to drive Sarah down to her mother's. She hated confrontations with Keith and hoped this could happen without his getting involved. Sarah dressed as Tracy packed a small overnight bag with her clothes.

"What are you doing, Mommy?"

"Do you think you can drive down to Grandma's with Caroline by yourself?"

"Of course, Mother. I'm seven."

"Excuse me. Of course you are."

"Why is Caroline going?" the girl asked as she brushed her hair.

"Because I am not going to be able to go. You're going. I talked with Grandma last night and she told me how much she missed you. So I thought you could go down and see her for a few days. I have work to do."

"Mother, I have to read my part in the Three Kings Play today..." Sarah said with increasing anxiety. "Sister Claire told us we had to be ready.... Does Daddy know I'm going?... We're supposed to have dinner tonight... Does Sister Anne know I won't be in class?" Sarah said with growing urgency.

"I'll call Sister Anne. Don't worry, this will all be arranged. Now hurry. Grandma is very anxious to see you; she wants you to help her bake a cake," Tracy said to her daughter.

"Oh, I know how to make a very good chocolate cake," Sarah replied.

"I know, that's why Grandma wants your help," Tracy said moving towards the door. "Now hurry. I have to get ready myself," she said, and went back into her bedroom.

While she was there the phone rang, and Sarah picked it up. She had only recently been allowed to answer it, and was very proud of being able to do so. It was her father.

"Daddy. Guess what? Mommy says I'm going to Grandma's.... she's in the shower. I don't know. In a few minutes I guess. We won't be able to have dinner. Bye. I love you too," Sarah said in a rush, then hung up the phone.

Tracy dressed as quickly as she could, and before she could really talk to Sarah, Michael was at the door.

"It's set up. Caroline just called me. She'll be here any minute in the center's Subaru" he said, as he took Sarah's bag and led her out. Caroline drove up just as the three of them came out of the building. Caroline transferred Tracy's instructions to the GPS and phone, then she got into the driver's seat.

Weldon pulled up in his pickup and parked in Barbara's handicapped space, and went down the ramp to her apartment. While he was inside Coyote arrived in his Mercedes convertible. A few minutes later Barbara and Weldon came back out and with a hydraulic lift. Weldon got Barbara into the truck and her wheelchair into the flatbed. It was clear they had done this before, and that he had rigged his truck so that he could do it. They bantered back and forth and the affection between them was obvious.

Coyote and Weldon got out and came over to where Michael was standing, and the three of them went through the plan again.

"We've each got a first airstrip, and if they don't check out, whoever is closest to the last two will do them; we each have information on all of them. We're texting as needed, and put your phone on vibrate. You might be in a tight place where sound would give you away. But remember, coverage is spotty so copy in Barbara, and check in with her every hour even if you have to move to get bars or find a landline. If she doesn't hear from one of us, she'll take it from there."

Weldon and Coyote affirmed they understood, then Coyote said, "I'm doing the airstrip near Winchester, Virginia."

"Have you ever been out there?" Michael asked.

"I've been as far as Leesburg," he answered. "It's a pretty town. Colonial, but no further than that. I looked at Google Earth, though, and I can see it's very rural." While they were speaking, Tracy was getting Sarah's safety belt set up. "Now... did you remember to bring Miss Pitts?"

"Of course, Mother. I couldn't leave her. She gets scared at night."

"I'm headed down into Maryland," Weldon said.

"Me too, Michael replied. "Remember to check in every hour." Then, turning to Weldon, "Barbara gave you the files?"

Weldon held up his tablet. "Got everything here. Dropping Barbara off at that French restaurant in the woods. Checking in every hour, starting at 10... right?"

As Michael was turning to leave, Caroline started the Subaru's engine and was about to pull out when Keith raced up, double parked, and got out of his car.

"What the hell do you think you're doing?" he said, his voice filled with anger.

"Hi Daddy. . ."

"What's going on, Tracy?"

Caroline turned the engine off and looked very confused and caught in the middle of something she didn't understand.

Tracy tried to sound reasonable when she responded, "I'm sending Sarah to my mother's for a few days. We talked about this."

"We talked about it, and I told you I forbade it. I got the injunction. You'll be served the notice this afternoon," Keith said, looking as if he was on the edge of violence. Caroline began to open her car door to get out.

Michael saw this and went over to where they stood. "Keith, let's not have a scene in the street."

"Dammit...I'm sure you're at the heart of this. Ever since you got involved with my wife there's been one problem after another. Well it's not happening," he said, and reached for the Subaru's door. "Come on Sarah... we're getting out of here."

While they had been arguing no one had noticed that Weldon had gotten out of his truck and had come to stand next to Michael and Tracy. Caroline, meanwhile, stood next the Subaru, very unsure what was happening.

"Tracy... maybe I shouldn't... maybe this isn't a good idea..." she said, sounding very stressed.

"Tracy feels Sarah needs to get out of town. That's what's going to happen," Weldon said.

The hostility and tension in the air made Sarah begin to cry.

"I see, Tracy. You've got this goon to back you up. Well it isn't going to work. I'm going to call Jack and find out what the court can do... and I'm calling the police." Turning to Michael with a sneer, he said, "You I could've taken care of alone. But I'm going to name you in this," Keith said as he got back into his car and drove away.

"I'm sorry that Mommy and Daddy had to fight, sweetheart. Sometimes adults don't have all the answers. Now come on," Tracy said as he pulled away.

"I don't want to go. Why is Daddy so mad...?"

"Tracy, ride down with her and come back and meet us,"

Before it all came unglued, Tracy looked at Caroline and said, "You have to trust me on this. This is really urgent. There are things Keith knows nothing about that I can't talk about. I wouldn't ask you to do this if it weren't an emergency. I need you to be the nurse you are."

Then turning to Sarah, who was gearing up for a tantrum, she said, "Sarah. I need a big girl now. Not a baby. I want you to go with Caroline to Grandma's. And I need for you to behave like a big girl now. Can you do that?"

Sarah snuffled and had tears in her eyes, but she felt her mother's urgency, and responded. Caroline did as well. She got back into the car, and the two of them drove off.

"We've each got about an hour and a half drive to our assigned airstrip, and Weldon also has to drop off Barbara. It's now eight o'clock. If we don't stop it in eight hours a nuclear bomb is going to destroy the capitol city of the United States. Tracy told me this whole thing sounds like fiction."

"Yeah," Weldon said, "Mission Impossible."

The three men first laughed, then embraced in a hug and separated.

Tracy and Michael got into his jeep. Weldon went back to his pick-up, and Coyote to his car. Michael, Tracy, and Coyote started out together. They went down to M Street and across the Key Bridge to the George Washington Parkway at which point Tracy, Michael and Weldon went onto the Interstate 495 ring highway towards Maryland, while Coyote got on Interstate 270, heading into West Virginia.

Weldon went up Massachusetts Avenue until he got to Mount Vernon Parkway. He was feeling very wired. He trusted Michael and Tracy, and Barbara especially. They saw him. Not his black skin, or his muscles, or his size, but him. They saw what he saw. It was a bond he had only experienced with White people in combat. So it never occurred to him to doubt what they were doing, and he didn't do so now. Instead he found himself mentally and emotionally hyped. It was adrenaline, he knew, and he welcomed it. He had lain awake last night allowing himself to sink into it. It was like combat again, being on patrol in a hot zone.

CHAPTER TWENTY-EIGHT

28 November — Rural Maryland

Weldon finally got onto Interstate 395 headed south, looking for Exit 7 onto Highway 295. He was headed for Fort Washington, Maryland, and he just let the GPS guide him. The airfield he was supposed to check was in rural Maryland, and there was another one he would check if the first three sites were duds. They were very far apart and they were in an area with which he was familiar, which is why he had asked for them. He had grown up in Friendly, a planned mostly African-American community not far away.

He and Barbara usually talked and listened to music. They had liked each other from the moment they met. He knew it seemed very improbable to others, except maybe Tracy and Michael, that a thirty-year-old Black housepainter, three tour combat veteran, and a fifty-five-year-old wheelchair-bound overweight red-headed Nobel laureate physicist could find much in common. But they could and did. She reminded him of his mother's aunt, his great aunt who was from the Bayou country near New Orleans, and who he and his mother had gone to visit several times when he was growing up. She had also been in a wheelchair so he was used to that. She had taught him how to play baccarat and backgammon, and they had played during humid summers during those visits.

Now he played with Barbara, and they were well matched. She appreciated, she had told him, that he was not intimidated by who she was and just hung out with her.

But that morning they didn't say much, each lost in their own thoughts. As they went down Livingston Road towards a small bay in the Potomac River to La Salle Du Bois, the farm-to-table restaurant owned by Michael's and Barbara's friend André.

As the bay came into view, Barbara turned and said to Weldon with great passion, "Now listen to me Weldon. I love you, and I don't want anything happening to you. You understand? This is like combat. I don't know what that is but I remember what you told me."

"I know Barb. I've been moving into it since last night. Don't worry."

He parked in the gravel lot in front of what had once been a typical center hall Maryland white clapboard farm house, but was now a destination restaurant with an international reputation.

As they were parking, Barbara said, "You know how I was introduced to this restaurant, Weldon?"

"No, how?"

"The foundation director that took me said Anthony Bourdain had come from New York just to have dinner."

"Not sure how to take that. I've seen video of Anthony Bourdain eating street food in Myramar made from pieces of things it would never occur to me could be eaten."

He got Barbara out of the truck and into her wheelchair, and walked behind her as she drove her chair up the ramp. André, the chef-owner, came out as they reached the top. He was in his late forties, a very elegant Frenchman in an offhand no special effort kind of way. He took Barbara's hand, leaned over and kissed her on both cheeks. "Professor, it is so nice to see you again."

"Hello André, this is my friend, Weldon Shelcraft. Weldon, this is André Pau, truly one of the great chefs," Barbara said.

Weldon and André took one another in, asked no questions, and just assumed that if they were each friends of Barbara's and Michael's, they would probably get along. They came to that conclusion at about the same time, and each put out his hand and they shook. André turned and led them inside, through the dining rooms and into a combination back office and sitting room that had wainscoting and a fireplace. On the walls were badly executed oil paintings of nude young women. One of them had clearly been painted in that very room.

"I must go back to work; *The Los Angeles Times* is coming for dinner tonight. They don't think I know that, but of course I do," André said, making a gesture with his hand. "It's the same woman who did the latest French Laundry review. Very fussy." He stopped at the door, "Excuse my manners, can I get you anything? The kitchen will make you anything you want."

"Just some coffee, André, thank you. Weldon isn't staying. But if you could make him one of those chicken, lettuce, brie and chutney sandwiches and give him a cup of coffee, I know he would appreciate it."

André and Weldon smiled at each other, recognizing they were both being manipulated in the nicest way. "But of course, very simple. Give me a moment."

When André left, Weldon gestured with his head toward one of the paintings, his question not needing to be spoken aloud.

"He's in a life study art program at the Academy," Barbara explained. "André decided he wanted to be painter. I've no idea why: he's not terribly good at it. But it is so completely different than the rest of his life, I think, it gives him an escape. It seems to be very stressful running a restaurant at this level."

"You would never know it from his manner though," Weldon said.

"No. He makes it look effortless; it's part of what makes him special," Barbara said.

"The girls?"

"They're all students with him. They do life modeling so they can have money to get through school, but it's not steady, and it's expensive to attend the academy. He hires them as waitresses to help out. Being a waitress at one of the world's great restaurants is about as steady an income as a waitress can get. I think he's booking two years in advance now. I am sure he sleeps with some of them, but whatever goes on is completely consensual."

"How do you know?"

"I've talked with them about it. Food is not the only thing André is loved for. In that world Le Salle Du Bois and André are legendary, paintings and all," Barbara said with a laugh, as Weldon unpacked the case that held her laptop, second screen, and her collapsible satellite dish to catch the signal. With his help she booted up her laptop and had just finished when André came back, handed a box to Weldon, with a smile saying there's more than Barb's sandwich in this. He also gave him an insulated metal wide-mouth bottle with several cups of coffee in it, and put a cup of coffee down in front of Barbara.

"It's 8:20, I gotta go," Weldon said as he thanked André and gave Barbara a hug. As soon as he was gone, André came over to Barbara and sat on the edge of the coffee table so they would be at eye level.

"I don't know what you are doing, but I can see it is serious, and not normal. Is there anything else I can do?"

"Nothing André. That you are doing this is a critical factor," Barbara said with a look of affection and tenderness.

"I'll leave you to it, then," André responded, and left.

As Weldon drove in the silence he found himself thinking about what would happen if they did not succeed. He had accepted, as he had in Afghanistan, as you had to, that he could die. You had to deal with that, accept it, and let it go. Not doing so put you at risk, biasing your actions and thoughts. It was different, though, when he thought about the city, the world, and what a nuclear explosion in Washington, D.C. would do. It was hard to comprehend. A million people might die.

He made a conscious effort to stop thinking about it as he turned onto Old Allentown Road and went down to Airport Drive. Off to his left, small as a penny, he could see the giant seaside ferris wheel for which the venerable town was known. Ft. Washington was just close enough for some people to commute, so like a lot of rural commuter towns to D.C., it was a mix of very old and brand-new houses. Out on the edge of the Potomac River was the historic stone and brick fort for which the town was named.

It was 9:45 when he drove onto the airfield grounds. There wasn't much to it, only one airstrip, no control tower.

A line of stanchions holding up metal roofs paralleled the landing strip. Sheltering beneath them were small single engine planes. On the other side were several weathered old metal hangars, looking like sagging double garages, a few with their doors up showing the planes within. Further out there were some small planes tied down on the revetment. Just off from the end of the hangars was a modular metal office. He parked on the tarmac in front of it; there was only one other car.

He went in and saw a blonde woman in her forties too big for her clothes. She looked up from the television on her desk and said rather suspiciously, "Can I help you?"

Weldon was used to the tone; all Black men were, and didn't let it bother him. He gave her a warm smile and went into the role she would accept. "My boss sent me down. Someone flew in on a small plane and I was supposed to meet him, but he never showed up." He took out the picture of the man Constance had seen in her session and showed it to the woman. "I don't have a picture, but my boss' daughter made this drawing the last time he was here."

The woman looked at it and shook her head, "Nah. Never seen him."

"Could I go down the line?" he asked, with another smile.

The woman had relaxed, but this question put her back on guard.

"You can walk the line, but you can't go into the hangars."

"I understand. Listen maybe I don't even have to do that. My boss remembered part of the tail number," he said, showing her his phone screen. "The boss is worried something happened to him. He didn't tell us which airport he was coming into."

"That plane's not here. Never been here, in fact. This isn't like Dulles you know. I remember planes because I know most of the ones that go in and out of here. This is a Flight Restricted Zone," she said, and when he looked puzzled, added, "This is in the Flight Restricted Zone, because of the government up in D.C.. You have to have a PIN license to land here."

"Well, thank you. You've been very helpful. I appreciate it," he responded, turned and left the office.

He went out and walked past all the planes just to be sure, but didn't expect to find anything. And he didn't. By then it was 10:45.

Weldon got into his car and at 11:00 pulled over onto the road's shoulder and checked in with Barbara. He told her he had been to the Fort Washington location, had found nothing, and was going up to Clinton to check Hansen field. In return Barbara told him that Tracy and Michael had checked the Harper's Ferry field and also found nothing. She had heard from Coyote he was headed toward his first field.

CHAPTER TWENTY-NINE

28 November — Rural Maryland

Coyote took the toll road 66 West until it became Highway 23, and then 17, and finally Highway 50. He knew it was going to take over an hour to get there. Ordinarily it would have been a lovely drive. The Mercedes was wonderful. Every time he got in it he thought about the reservation, and the mesa's poverty. When he was living there he hadn't really thought of it so much as poverty; it was just the way you and everyone you knew lived.

In high school he had been selected to be sent to Washington at the request of the state's senior senator, who wanted a Native American page in the Senate. His father, who was the Chief, and the Shaman both came to him one afternoon with the proposition, and he had agreed.

At sixteen, a junior with a 4.0 GPA in his school, he had boarded a bus and taken it from Flagstaff to Washington. He was good in school because he had learned early that adults would leave you alone if you had decent grades. He disliked D.C. from the first. He hated the confinement, the waiting, and being at the beck and call of the Senators and their staffs. When he saw them close up he found many of them shallow and corrupt. He went to the page high school and finished cum laude, which got him a free ride at George Washington University. The whole time he was there he felt he was a kind of novelty. Everyone was very sensitive about Native Americans, and he was not only an Indian, he was a Hopi, a tribe Whites seemed to feel particularly favorable towards.

He joined the Sierra Club so he could learn where the trails were so he could get away from the White world. It was at a Sierra Club meeting that he met the hat check girl at the club where has was now the star D.J.. It was like playing a part, a kind of Kachina dance he did. He was consciously in costume, like the Kachina dancers. He saw the whole thing as an exercise in changing consciousness. To mold minds to the world he lived in, one that was a matrix of consciousness.

To his great pleasure it paid extraordinarily well. His indulgence was his car; much of the rest he sent back, split between the reservation's elementary school and the Indian Health Service Hopi Health Care Center.

As he drove through the green and wooded farmlands and turned onto county 624, he admitted to himself that for all his success he had been lonely. Meeting Michael and the others, and particularly Weldon, had given him a non-Indian family, and the kind of closeness he had never felt before in the White world. The Hill Center people were linked at a deeper level than race or religion, as powerful as those connections were. What bonded them was the open inclusion of nonlocal consciousness in each of their lives. Michael had created a safe haven where the experience of non-ordinary consciousness was not only tolerated, it was encouraged. It was what they talked about and thought about, And he deeply appreciated that it did not come with any religious overlay that tried to convert him from his culture and faith.

Shortly after he pulled onto 628 he saw the sign for the airstrip. There was hardly anything to it. It wasn't even paved.

Just a long grassy strip of land with trees a short distance back on either side. He parked the Mercedes and got out, putting his Glock 9 between his back and his pants.

No one seemed to be around. There were only a few metal garage-like structures, open on one long side to face the field. In one he could see a red and white biplane. As he walked down the grass with the hangars on either side, he saw that all the planes looked like something from World War I, or not much later. It was easy to check their numbers, but he had the sense as he did so that this was a waste of time. This was not the airstrip.

He had just walked past the last hangar when a beat up green Ford pick-up drove up. A middle-aged man dressed like a farmer got out and came over to him.

"Can I help you young man?"

"I'm trying to find out what has happened to a friend of mine," Coyote answered.

"I don't understand."

"He has a plane, kind of like that red and white one over there, and he was flying it up from Richmond. The message was garbled at the end and I couldn't understand where he was going to land. I can't reach him and I'm worried something has happened."

"You an Indian?"

Coyote was caught off guard by the question. "Yes, I am, The Hopi are my people."

"Thought so. Nice car."

"Yes it is. Look, he obviously isn't here, so I am going to go on."

"That's good," the man said, and watched until Coyote got into his car and started to drive off. Then he got in his truck.

Coyote drove back down the road, pulled over onto the shoulder near some woods, and called Barbara.

She had heard from Tracy and Michael, and Weldon; all their first airports produced nothing.

"It's getting late. Are they going to do the other two, then?" he asked.

"Yes."

"All right, I will head over that way and check in when I get closer, but it is going to take me several hours."

"I know, I can see," Barbara answered. "But I think that's the right move. Have you tried texting them?

"Yes, but it's not getting through."

"Well, we're in contact so I will call you or text you if anything comes up."

CHAPTER THIRTY

28 November — Rural Maryland

Hansen field was another single strip with no control tower. It was significantly more run down than the Ft. Washington field, with several obviously dead aircraft tied down, one with ivy growing up the landing gear.

A line of metal garage hangars paralleled the runway, then further off were stanchions with roofing under which several planes were tied down. Even further down the runway was another section of hangars. A metal modular office was just a short way in from the turnoff, and Weldon parked there. He could see a lone man working on a plane at the furthest hangar.

He went into the office, and a wiry man in his 60s with a veteran's baseball cap was sitting behind the counter reading a clipboard. He looked up when Weldon came in.

"Can I help you?" Weldon told him the same story he had told the woman in Ft. Washington, about a lost business contact, and showed him the drawing. He was electrified when the man gestured down to the hangars.

"I'm not sure it's the same guy, but he looks just like that,' the man said. "Anyway he's there; at least he was earlier, and I haven't seen him drive off."

"Thank you," Weldon said, and walked out to his truck, not sure what his next move should be. He got back into his truck and decided to watch for a moment. He took a pair of binoculars out of the glove compartment and looked down at the hangar where he had seen the man working, although he wasn't there now. He thought he saw someone look out, but the movement was so fast he couldn't be sure. He decided it was essential that he get his location back to the others, so he rang Barbara and told her what he had seen.

"They have no reason to expect me, or that I would know anything about what they were doing. They don't want to attract attention, I don't think."

"Weldon, maybe you should wait until you get some backup," Barbara responded.

"We don't have time. If this is a dead end like the last one, we'll lose too much time. But for sure let Michael and Tracy know," he answered.

"I agree, but be alert," Barbara said, and for the first time her tone was deadly serious. "I'll get this to Michael and Tracy. Coyote is too far away, on the other side of the Potomac."

Inside the hangar, Farouk and Moustapha were working with great intensity. The bomb case was open. Nestled inside was the metal sphere. Farouk climbed into the small single-engine plane and removed a gray aluminum partition in the back. It revealed a small space where the frame of the plane could be seen, like the spine and rib cage of a primordial beast. With the panel removed he got out and went over to the bomb in its case. Moustapha handed Farouk a box marked "Kryton Triggers."

Farouk took one of the triggers from the box; it looked like a small old-fashioned vacuum tube. Also from the box he took a band of explosive material packed in a belt. These conventional shaped charges were the trigger. When they went off all together it detonated the nuclear blast. Moustapha handed him a caulking gun with a tube of Flex Glue. He put the belt around the sphere, holding it in place with evenly spaced squirts from the glue gun. Then Moustapha reached into the case and took out a small box of electronics with a clock read-out, and handed it to Farouk, who connected that to the belt with a USB cable.

He opened the electronics box, checked the battery, and finding everything okay, he carefully inserted the trigger into the circuit board. He attached that to the electric timer and then to the battery. The clock lit up, showing a red display. He looked at his watch; it was 12:13. He set the timer for current time. Then he flipped a switch opening the circuit. He set the count down for 3 p.m. and closed the box.

With Moustapha's help he got the sphere positioned to put in the space he had opened by taking out the panel. Using his caulking gun he secured the box to the sphere and then to the aircraft. Finally, he and Moustapha put this whole assemblage in the space behind the partition, and with more squirts he secured it to the plane frame. He carefully screwed back the panel and put the rear seat cushion back in place. The bomb was entirely invisible.

"It is activated. No matter what happens, and no matter where, it goes off at three." Farouk said.

"Does Said...," Moustapha began.

"He's asleep at the motel. I put something in his coffee. We need him to be rested. I'll wake him about two. He does not even know where the bomb is hidden. Washington, D.C. is about to become history, Inshalla."

After he hung up with Barbara, Weldon looked down the airstrip again, working out what he was going to do. He started up his engine and drove down the line of planes, checking their numbers against his number with the plan of blocking the hangar exit so the plane could not take off. When he got positioned he reached under the seat and pulled out his Sig Sauer P320, checked the magazine, jacked in a round, and put a second magazine in one jacket pocket and the Sig Sauer in the other. At this point emotionally he was in Afghanistan poised for battle.

The hangar door was partially open, and he could see a man, clearly of middle eastern heritage, sitting in a chair apparently oblivious of him. As Weldon watched him the man looked up, seemingly unconcerned.

Weldon walked up to Moustapha and showed him the picture. "Have you seen this man around here?" he asked.

"No. There's a doctor who has a plane a bit further down who looks... but no. I'm sorry I can't help you," Moustapha said, affecting a Brooklyn accent.

Weldon nodded and started to turn, and as he did so, he saw the tail numbers of the plane in the hangar. At just that moment another truck pulled up and the two men who had brought the bomb saw Weldon and both immediately got out of the truck. The older one had a gun in his hand. Both came towards Weldon in a very threatening way.

"Nigger, you got a problem," the younger man said, and reached out to Weldon, who grabbed his arm and swung him into the other man, knocking the gun out of his hand. Weldon hit the older one in the throat with his knuckled hand, which dropped him instantly, leaving him gasping.

The younger man broke away, reached down and picked up a hammer from the tools next to the plane, and swung it at Weldon, who grabbed it and followed its momentum, pulling the younger man off his feet and slamming him into the ground, knocking him unconscious. He heard the cocking of a gun and dropped to the ground as a bullet went past him so close he could hear it. He grabbed the screw driver Farouk had used to take out the panel, and threw it as you would a knife. It caught Moustapha in the belly. It didn't penetrate very far, but far enough to cause so much pain, the next two shots Moustapha got off were way off to the left.

Weldon picked up the hammer and before Moustapha could fire again he struck his arm with the hammer, sending the gun flying through the air.

Unseen by Weldon while he was struggling with Moustapha, Farouk had come out of the hangar office and slipped behind him, holding a shovel he had found leaning up in a corner of the small room. He clubbed Weldon on the side of the head as hard as he could, and Weldon dropped to the ground.

"Good, God," Moustapha said, holding his shirt up and looking at his abdomen and the bleeding wound caused by the screwdriver, then at his arm. "Who is this man? He has a drawing of you, Farouk."

Farouk leaned over Weldon and rifled through his pockets, pulling out the printout with the remote viewing session drawing. Looking at it, he said, "How can this be? Nobody but a handful of people know what I look like since the surgery."

Farouk pulled out Weldon's Sig Sauer. He checked to see a round was in the chamber, then reached in his back pocket and took out his wallet. Holding the gun he pulled out credit cards and the driver's license.

"Weldon Shelcraft. Nothing official. There's a card that says he is a housepainter. None of this makes any sense. No one... no one, Moustapha, knows about the bomb... or about us. How could they know what I look like now?" he said as Moustapha got the first aid kit out of the plane and dressed his wound.

"Farouk, if there is anyone in the airstrip office we have to assume they probably heard the shots, although they may not know where they came from. We're in the hangar so they may have sounded far away. They won't see us because of the truck of those infidel nazi fools."

""The timeline has changed..." Farouk interrupted. Looking down at the two White militia men, he said, "Those two infidels will come to in a while. I'd kill them but we need their militia's help to get where the boat picks us up."

As they had been talking the two militia men were recovering.

'What the fuck is going on here," Darrell, the younger man said.

"We don't know. We have no idea why this man is here," Farouk answered.

"Is he some kind of police?" The older man asked in a husky scratchy voice.

"His wallet says he's a housepainter."

"A house painter... look at him. He's some kind of soldier. I can tell you he has been trained to fight. Somebody is on to you. You better speed things up."

"I agree," Farouk responded. "But it doesn't make any sense. A lone soldier comes randomly to this hangar in rural Maryland. Your people picked this field because it was so out of the way. Why would he be here? What could he have seen? Before you got here, what was there to see?" Farouk demanded. "A middle-aged man, speaking in a Brooklyn accent sitting in a chair reading. Obviously working on his innocuous looking plane, so not planning to fly anywhere. Why would that attract any attention? Yet he saw something."

"And why would he have a picture of you, Farouk?" Mustapha added, and Farouk gave him a venomous look for revealing that information to the militia men.

"We must put this aside until later," he said, walking back to the office. I will call Said. He can be here very quickly. As we planned, we will abandon his car."

"Yes, and we drive you to the Aqualand Marina, down the 301."

"Yes, we'll continue as planned." Standing in the doorway of the office, Farouk turned to Moustapha, "I want you to drive the Black man's truck. Go to that picnic bench by the side of the road. You know the one, next to the stream. Here's his gun," he said, handing the weapon to Moustapha. "Kill him. Make it look like suicide. You wait there for Said. I'll tell Said to drive that way. Leave the man's truck. Come back with Said. He's just a man who killed himself. Why would anyone connect it with us, with this airstrip? We're down to hours and need to get Said in the air," he said, thought for a moment, and added, "When we leave," he said to the older militia man, "can one of you kill the man behind the counter? Take the security videos."

Moustapha nodded his agreement, "Nobody knows us. Nobody connects us. The plane is in Said's American name."

Moustapha loaded Weldon into the truck and got behind the wheel. He drove about ten miles further into the countryside until he saw the old-fashioned wayside stop with a cement picnic bench overlooking a bubbling creek.

There was a picnic table, a trash bin, and an old aluminum phone booth with the glass broken out on one side and the telephone handset dangling from its cable. Weldon was coming to. Moustapha gestured with the gun but he had to help Weldon get out, and he fell to the ground when he did. Moustapha pointed towards the picnic table and Weldon got up and staggered to the bench and sat down. The truck shielded the two men from being visible to the road.

"Who are you?" Moustapha asked.

"Weldon Shelcraft."

"Please.... do not lie, infidel. Who do you work for?"

"I'm a house painter. Self-employed."

"I regret I do not have time for such games," Moustapha responded, looking at his watch which showed 1 p.m. "It does not matter anyway."

He raised the Sig Sauer just as Weldon threw the handful of gravel he had scooped up when he stumbled, into Moustapha's face. It caused Moustapha to flinch, and his first shot went wide. Instantly, he fired again and the range was so close the bullet grazed the side of Weldon's already damaged head, tearing through his cheek and blowing off much of his left ear. He slumped over the picnic bench with blood pouring out of the wound.

Moustapha walked over and looked down at him as he wiped the gun with his handkerchief. He searched Weldon's clothes systematically and took out the drawing of Farouk and put it in his own pocket. He put the gun in Weldon's hand, wrapped his fingers around, and fired it again so the forensic technicians would find that he had fired a gun.

He ejected the clip from the Sig Sauer, got the second magazine out of Weldon's jacket, took two rounds from it, added them to the gun's magazine, and reinserted it. The second magazine he put in his pocket. It would look like Weldon had committed suicide, one bullet fired.

As he was doing this, Said pulled into the waystop.

"Farouk told me to meet you here."

"Yes. Let's go."

"Is he dead?" Said asked, pointing to Weldon.

"Not quite but he will be shortly. He committed suicide; I don't know why." Moustapha said with a grim laugh.

Both got into the rental SUV and drove back to the airfield. It was 1:45.

CHAPTER THIRTY-ONE

28 November — Rural Maryland

Barbara was still sitting in André's office. The clock read 1:45, and she was frantic. No one had checked in. Suddenly her phone rang.

"Oh, God. Michael. What's going on? Do you have any idea how crazy I am.... a flat tire… no cell service. You're kidding."

"We went to the airstrip. No plane with that number was there. What else have you heard?

"Like the one you and Tracy went to, Coyote's strip in Virginia was a dead end. He's on his way over to Maryland because you all and Tracy are there. But it will take him hours to get there."

"What about Weldon?"

"The first place he went he found nothing. He called a few minutes ago from the airfield in Clinton. He thought he saw something, was going to call back. But he hasn't. I have been trying to call him but all I get is his voice mail, and he doesn't answer texts."

Tracy was listening on the speaker and put her hand on Michael's arm. "We have go there. I think something has happened to Weldon."

"Did you hear that Barb? We're going to go directly to Clinton."

As they hung up André came into the office.

"How's it going, Professor?"

"It's making me crazy. I think something's happened to our friend Weldon and I'm not sure what to do."

"Call the police."

"You're right."

Barbara went to her computer and set up a call that could not be traced. When it was answered, she said, "Listen carefully. I'm only going to say this once. I have information which tells me a bomb has been planted at the Clinton, Maryland General Aviation airstrip. It is set to go at 3 this afternoon, and I believe it may be in a small plane whose tail number is N769." Then she broke the connection and noted the time. It was 1:50. Whatever was going to happen was going to do so in 70 minutes.

As Barbara sat in the restaurant, Michael and Tracy raced down Interstate 495 and onto State Route 5, following the GPS. This routed them to a county road; as they were going down it towards the airstrip, they passed the wayside stop.

"Stop. Go back! "Tracy shouted, and Michael jammed on the brakes.

"I'm sure that's Weldon's truck back there."

Michael backed up a couple hundred yards until he was facing Weldon's truck, and pulled off onto the wayside. They saw no other vehicles, and no one was around. They didn't see Weldon, but they parked, got out and ran to the truck, saw there was no one in it, and turned and looked down the hill by the creek. They saw Weldon's body slumped over the old concrete picnic table and ran down to him. He lay in a pool of blood from a head wound. When Michael gently nudged him he did not respond. Looking down at him, Tracy said, "There is a gun in his hand."

"A Sig Sauer?" Michael asked, not looking up.

"I don't know one gun from another." She reached down to pick it up.

Michael caught her movement and said, "Don't touch it." Then he bent closer and put his fingers on Weldon's carotid artery. "He's not dead, but I don't know how bad it is. You can see it's a head wound. It took off his ear. It was made to look like a suicide, I think. No one would connect this with the airstrip miles away. Why would they?"

"We don't know how long he's been here," Tracy said.

Michael ran back to his jeep and got out his first aid kit, then went to Weldon's truck and got his. He took it down to Tracy, who was talking to 911, giving her longitude and latitude coordinates and telling them what they had found.

"Sorry, I have to get off the phone to take care of this man. Get here as quick as you can."

When she hung up she opened the first aid kits, and with the basic first aid skills anyone who spends a lot of time in wilderness or remote places has to learn, she started to dress his wounds. "Go. This doesn't require both of us."

"You're right, I'm off," Michael said. "Given that all the data saw this happening in D.C., if my calculations are right they have to take off in about twenty-five minutes. I can just make it.... maybe."

They looked into each other's eyes, both knowing it might be the last time they ever saw one another. They embraced for a moment and kissed with the tenderness of finality.

As Michael turned to leave, he said, "Call Barbara. Tell her what's happening." Then he was in the jeep and off, speeding into the distance headed towards the Clinton airstrip. Fifteen minutes later he went through the open chain link gate and down to the office. He jumped out of the jeep and ran into the modular building. The man behind the counter, without even being asked, pointed towards the hangars, and Michael ran out. He suddenly realized that what he had thought were a couple of deer hunters in the nearby woods, a not unfamiliar sound during deer season, might have been something else. He reached for his phone and dialed 911.

Michael looked down the hangar line, and at the last hangar could see the door being pushed open. He jumped back into his jeep and raced towards the hangar. Just as he got there the plane began to taxi out and line up to go down the runway. Michael steered the jeep parallel to the plane and then wrenched the wheel to the right, forcing the small plane off the runway and onto the earthen verge. The force of the jeep's momentum crumpled the struts on the pilot's side which caused the left wing of the plane to partially collapse.

Looking back in his side mirror, Michael saw several men rush out of the hangar and begin firing some kind of military rifles at him. His side mirror disintegrated as a bullet hit it; another struck his dashboard. As this was happening he heard sirens come screaming onto the airfield. When he turned to look back, a SWAT team poured out of the back of one of the vehicles. Overhead a news helicopter hovered.

Moustapha and Farouk fell to the ground, hit by multiple bullets from the SWAT team, then the two militia men hiding behind the truck were hit. Another helicopter, this one black and governmental, suddenly came in from the left, forcing the news copter out of the way.

In the small plane Said pulled out a pistol and fired at Michael, hitting him in his shoulder. Michael was so charged with adrenalin that at first he didn't even feel it. He rolled out of the jeep as Said fired again, the bullet missing him by inches. He hit the ground and the jarring impact caused the wound in his shoulder to flare up. He was consumed with exquisite pain and blacked out for a moment. When he came to he was surrounded by the SWAT team pointing their weapons at him and shouting, "Hands behind your back."

He tried to comply but his wounded arm would not do it. The police seemed as confused as Michael as to what was actually going on, and they were becoming increasingly agitated. They didn't seem to register Said because he had sunk to below the window level of the plane. He bobbed up and began to fire, killing two of the SWAT team. He died in a blast of bullets that jerked his body first one way then another.

The black helicopter landed, and Sam Kassimir, Waterman, and Garth poured out. Kassimir had a bull horn in his hand and bellowed into it.

"Stand down. Everyone stand down. Leave that man on the ground alone." The police were so wired that it took them a moment to respond properly. Two of them pointed their weapons at Kassimir, who didn't flinch and yelled, "Put your damn weapons down. Now. Do you hear me. Now." This last was said with such vehemence it finally broke through the SWAT teams adrenalin high, and they did as ordered.

Garth ran over to where Michael lay on the ground.

"Michael are you all right? What's going on here?"

"What time is it?"

"It's two fifty one," Garth answered, looking at his watch.

"We have less than ten minutes to find it before it goes off."

"Before what goes off?" the ranking SWAT officer shouted.

"A five kiloton nuclear bomb," Michael responded, and saw the shock of his statement drain the blood from the SWAT team's faces.

"Where is it?"

"I don't know," Michael answered as he got to his feet.

A rage of noise arose as many voices clamored with questions.

"Shut up. Would everyone please just shut up for a minute and let me think," Michael shouted, and the intensity of his intent commanded.

The voices stopped, but the highly agitated men began looking everywhere.

Michael closed his eyes and tried to remember everything he had been told in the remote viewing sessions. There was something just on the edge of his awareness.

He looked at Garth. "It has to be in the plane." They rushed forward together to the plane and pulled out Said's dead body.

"Where could something like this be?" Garth shouted, pulling the seat forward. There was nothing to see. It was two fifty three.

"It has to be behind the rear seat," Michael said, tearing the back of the rear seat out, revealing nothing but the blank wall against which the seat had rested.

"It has to be in there," he said, climbing into the plane and kicking the panel with his feet. After a moment it crumpled and he pulled it out. In the small dark space suddenly exposed, he saw the bomb sphere, the trigger-belt, and the gray electronics box with a read-out showing, "2:57."

Garth had climbed into the plane on the other side, and together they cut and pulled so that they could wrench the belt and the control box from the sphere; its read-out showed 2:59.

It finally gave way. Michael grabbed it, ran out into the field and threw the belt and the box as far as he could. In mid-air seconds later there was a large explosion as the trigger went off, and the belt and box were reduced to shrapnel. One piece of which flew past his head, missing him by inches.

Michael suddenly felt light-headed and almost collapsed. He realized he had been running entirely on adrenaline, and that there was blood running down his arm and his left shoulder didn't operate properly. Suddenly he was in a lot of pain. As he bent over in pain, an EMT came up to him and led him back to an ambulance. It had driven in without his even noticing it.

"Take off your shirt; can you do that?"

He could not get it off so the EMT took out scissors and cut with practiced ease. As the medic cleaned and dressed the wound, Michael looked around and saw there were more than twenty people around him, gathered in clusters. But then his attention was claimed by Coyote pulling up in his Mercedes. Coyote saw Michael sitting in the back of the ambulance and got out of his car and ran towards him. One of the SWAT team ran over to block him.

"Let him through," Michael shouted, and the man pulled back and let Coyote through. All around them people were at work. One group over by the plane were examining the bomb itself. Another group was around the bodies of Moustapha and Farouk. A third group was around the two White militia men. A fourth group, he realized, were media with their cameras, being held at bay by some of the SWAT team. It was a kind of controlled chaos; he was not sure what to do, and was suddenly very tired.

Kassimir, Waterman, and Garth came over to him and got there just as Coyote did. He stood a short distance away as the three men went over to Michael. For a moment no one spoke as they watched the medic finish.

Then Garth broke the silence. "Michael, this is Sam Kassimir, the head of the task force searching for the bomb, and Peter Waterman, another associate."

Michael gestured with his good hand, "A pleasure to meet you. As long as we're doing introductions," he said, and gestured Coyote over, "This is Istaqa Chester, one of the remote viewers who provided the information that saved Washington, D.C."

The three government men turned and looked at him with a kind of disbelief. Then Kassimir had the courtesy to say "Thank you," and put out his hand, which Coyote shook.

"We need to get you to the hospital and have this X-rayed and properly treated," the medic interrupted.

"Wait," Michael said. Looking at Coyote he asked, "Do you know what has happened with Weldon? He was shot."

"Tracy checked in with Barbara," Coyote answered. "He was taken to the Fort Washington Medical Center. She followed in his truck. He's in pretty bad shape."

"Who is Weldon?" Kassimir asked, "and why was he shot?"

"He's another viewer. He's part of our team; his sessions were what told me where to look for the bomb. He and Coyote were also part of the search team," Michael explained. Then he turned back to Coyote.

"Did Tracy tell you what happened?"

"She said they made it look like a suicide. The EMTs that came to get him knew nothing about any of this. They thought he was a suicide. She didn't know what was going on with you, so she just told them she was driving by saw him and pulled over."

"You say he's in Fort Washington Medical Center?" Kassimir asked.

"Yes," Coyote responded.

"Peter," Kassimir said, "Have Weldon airlifted to Walter Reed."

"He's a three-tour veteran," Coyote said, proud of his friend whom he saw as a gentle warrior.

"Even better; it will make the paperwork simpler," Kassimir replied.

Waterman walked back to the government helicopter.

"Listen, Coyote, drive up to André's and get Barbara. I know she will want to go to Walter Reed."

"Would that be Barbara Strickland, Michael?"

"It would. She was our command post at the La Salle du Bois."

"You had a Nobel Laureate physicist as your communications officer, and she was parked at one of the world's best restaurants? Do I have that right?" Kasimir asked.

"Yes, exactly," Michael responded.

"And what do you do, Coyote? I almost hesitate to ask."

"I'm a DJ at a club on M Street in Georgetown."

"You just couldn't make this up," Kassimir said, and laughed, and they all joined in. "Michael, when this is all over, I would love to hear how all these people, each so very different, came together. But right now let's get you out of here. We'll take you to Andrews. The doctors at the base will know how to deal with this, and you won't be harassed by media. Is he okay to go?" he said to the medic, who nodded.

With the help of Coyote, Michael followed Kassimir to the helicopter. When they got there Michael said to Coyote, "Call Tracy and tell her what's happening with me, and that she should go to the center so there is somebody there. I'm sure people will be checking in."

"Weldon Shelcraft will be airlifted to Walter Reed as soon as they have him stabilized," Waterman said to them all.

"Did you come in that jeep," Kassimir asked, and when Michael nodded, added "Are your keys still in it?"

"Yes," Michael answered.

"Good. Jake can drive it home for you," he said, beckoning to Garth who came over.

The helicopter was off, and Michael lay back against the seat, exhausted as the high of danger drained away. He was very tired, had never been more tired.

They flew him to Andrews Air Force Base, put him on a gurney, drove him to the hospital, and checked him in. They told him they would be back the next day.

"Not to worry, Michael," Kassimir told him as they took him into the hospital. "It will all be handled," he added.

As Michael was flying back, Coyote got in his car, called Tracy and told her what was happening and where Michael was going, and that he was going to get Barbara and take her to Walter Reed.

As he was driving up the road he called Barbara, who had just heard from Tracy. Her first words were, "Can you come get me? I need to get to Walter Reed."

"I know, I'm headed your way. I'll be there in half an hour."

When he got to the restaurant, Barbara was waiting, ready to go. Try as they might though there was no way they could get her electric wheelchair into the convertible.

"Don't worry, professor. It will fit in the van. I will have it delivered to your home tomorrow morning," André said as he helped her into the car.

"Thank you, André, thank you for everything," Barbara answered.

"And Walter Reed... there'll be lots of wheelchairs there," Coyote said, and they all laughed.

As they drove to Bethesda, Maryland, and the Walter Reed National Military Medical Center, Coyote and Barbara shared their experiences and put a picture together as best they could of what had just happened. As they were entering the Walter Reed grounds, Tracy checked in to say she was driving Weldon's truck and would join them as soon as she could. They told her what had happened with Michael, where he was, and what he wanted her to do.

When Coyote and Barbara arrived they found that instructions about them had been sent by Waterman. A wheelchair was waiting. Weldon was not there yet and it would be almost an hour before the helicopter landed. When it landed he was wheeled on a gurney into the emergency room for a first exam, then taken up to a room, where they were allowed to go.

Weldon at this point was awake but groggy. Coyote seeing the two of them, was sensitive enough to say, "I haven't eaten anything for hours. Why don't you stay with him Barbara while I find a place to get something."

As Coyote turned to leave a male nurse came into the room. "Sergeant, we're going to take you into surgery as soon as the orthopedic surgeon who specializes in your kind of gun wound arrives. The anesthesiologist will be in to see you in half an hour," he said, and left.

Finally, when they were alone, Barbara wheeled herself closer to Weldon. He reached out and she took his hand in both of hers.

"I told you to take care, and look what you've done," she said in mock chastisement.

"Yeah, well, you should see the other guys," Weldon said and drew her hands up and kissed them, something he had never done before.

"You know, when they told me you were shot, I thought I was going to lose you. Please don't ever do that to me again."

"You'll get no argument from me," he said although it was hard to understand him because his speech was slurred as a result of his wounds and the drugs they had given him. "In the future I promise I will do my best not to get shot," Weldon responded "Three tours without a scratch, but shot at a picnic table in rural Maryland. Who could predict such a thing?"

Barbara pushed herself up a bit and kissed Weldon on the lips as he lay on his uninjured side, then sank back and took his hand again. They sat there in silence just looking at one another.

CHAPTER THIRTY-TWO

29 November — Rural Maryland

Michael awoke the next morning feeling stiff and sore. He had an IV in his arm, which he only dimly remembered being inserted, and a desperate need to take a leak. Very gingerly he got out of bed, taking the IV bag on its wheeled stalk with him into the bathroom. When he came out, a nurse, Kassimir, Garth, and Tracy were in the room. She ran to him and embraced him.

"Weldon's alive, although if the bullet had gone half an inch to the left he wouldn't be. He lost part of his ear and his cheek is going to need some reconstructive work. That's why there was so much blood when we found him. They have him in surgery at Walter Reed right now. He's also got a skull fracture from a blow to the head, and a bad concussion, but he will be fine," Tracy said. "It's thanks to Dr. Kassimir that he was taken to Walter Reed. They do the best gunshot wound reconstruction work in the world, I'm told," Tracy said looking at Kassimir, who nodded in affirmation.

"When can I leave?" Michael asked, looking at the nurse.

"I think you will be discharged tomorrow," she answered.

Michael turned back to Tracy, "What about Coyote and Barbara?"

"He went back to André's as you asked him, got Barbara, and took her to Walter Reed. Then he drove to Walter Reed this morning. She wanted to be there when Weldon woke up," Tracy told him, then added, "I did as you asked and went back to the center. I've checked in with all the viewers and given them a very small synopsis of what happened. I didn't know how much I could say," she said, looking at Kassimir.

Then she took his hand and in a more stressed tone, "Everyone's okay, but it's a mess. Keith is suing me; Karen says you've received notification of your ethics hearing; the Hill Foundation has sent you something; and the front of the center is nothing but media vans. They're also in front of your house and the neighbors are complaining," Tracy said, hugging him again to take some of the sting out of her words. "You're both a hero and a villain; it's just crazy."

"Can someone at least get me a bathrobe?" Michael asked, suddenly feeling very exposed with nothing but his open-back hospital gown. Tracy went to the bathroom and brought one back.

"Can we take the IV out?" he said to the nurse.

"No, but I will show you how we can do it. Sit down," she answered, and he did so. She took the IV bag and threaded it through the arm of the robe; Michael stood up again, and the nurse helped him into the robe because his shoulder was still not cooperating. Then they hung the bag back on its hook.

He sat back down on his bed and looked at Kassimir.

"Michael, first let me say that your government, your country, in fact I think it is fair to say, the world, owes you and your team a great debt. You were right and we were wrong. That said I wish that had remained private. But the police got an anonymous tip, and to marshal their forces as quickly as possible put it out on their radio net, where the media picked it up. The whole thing was broadcast live and had a bigger audience than the O.J. slow motion chase. You and your team have been the subject of non-stop media coverage ever since, and I don't anticipate it will stop for quite a while."

"Well it seems I am about to lose my funding and my tenure, so that may end it."

"We've already talked to the Hill Foundation people, and that's not going to happen. In fact, your funding is about to go up because Health and Human Services, and the NIH are going to give you long-term grants."

"Really? Why would they do that?"

"Because we asked them to. Whatever it is you're doing, and I still don't understand it, it obviously works, and we support what works," Kassimir said, adding, "and you don't need to worry about the ethics hearing. We have had a conversation with Dr. Goldman and Dean Hopple, and you will receive notice tomorrow that it was all a misunderstanding. The charge has been withdrawn, and the issue has been dropped by the university and all records expunged."

Turning to Tracy, he said, "We can't do anything about your lawsuit, but given the positive publicity you are going to get because of some anonymous leaking to the media, I don't think it will be a problem. If Keith continues and you need some help, Jake will be happy to testify on your behalf, although I don't think it will come to that. I hate publicity," Kassimir said with real passion.

Michael started to ask questions, but Kassimir held up his hand.

"Leave it for now. They're going to let you go home tomorrow. You won't be bothered until then, and I recommend you and Tracy and her daughter go somewhere quiet for a few days. We have a lovely estate a short distance from Winchester, Virginia, and you are welcome to stay there. You won't be bothered. The media is going to be all over this for maybe a week of news cycles. While you're there, figure out what you want to say. To tell you the truth, we need some time to think that through as well. The White House has been fully briefed, and I think you're going to hear from the President. They want to keep the nuclear aspect out of it; just the usual terrorist bomb. Can you do that? Nuclear would just cause a panic."

"Of course," Michael said looking at Tracy.

"Yes, of course," she affirmed. "I will talk with everyone at the center."

"Good, thank you. We'll just put out that two of you were injured and we'll hold a press conference in a few days when you're able. Jake will help you with anything you need. Next week come see me; Jake will arrange it. You and your people have done something rather special, Michael, and I'd like to ask you to look at several little problems that are bothering us at the moment. But for now, just take it easy." With that, Kassimir and Garth left the room, and Tracy and Michael were alone for the first time.

They embraced again and kissed. When they drew apart Tracy said, "Our world is different now. I don't know if it will ever be the same."

"Probably not. But we have each other and everyone else is okay, so I am sure it will be an interesting adventure."

ACKNOWLEDGEMENTS

Once again I thank my wife Ronlyn, my partner and love who, in countless ways, makes my life better than it would otherwise be. I also thank Holly Thomas, whose copy editing polished the manuscript and meant a lot to me, and author Rob Swigart for his much appreciated suggestions.

AUTHOR BIO

Scientist, futurist, and award-winning author Stephan A. Schwartz is the columnist for the journal Explore, and editor of the daily Schwartzreport.net. For more than 40 years he has done consciousness research, and is one of the founders of Remote Viewing, and the anthropology of consciousness. He is the 2017 recipient of the Parapsychological Association's Outstanding Contribution Award. Current academic and research appointments: Distinguished Consulting Faculty of Saybrook University, Fellow of the William James Center for Consciousness Studies, Sofia University, and a Research Associate of the Cognitive Sciences Laboratory of the Laboratories for Fundamental Research. Prior academic appointments: Senior Samueli Fellow for Brain, Mind and Healing of the Samueli Institute; BIAL Fellow; founder and Research Director of the Mobius laboratory; Executive Director of the Rhine Research Center; and Senior Fellow of The Philosophical Research Society. Government appointments: Special Assistant for Research and Analysis to the Chief of Naval Operations, consultant to the Oceanographer of the Navy. Author of more than 130 technical reports and papers, 22 academic book chapters, and four books: *The Secret Vaults of Time, The Alexandria Project, Mind Rover, Opening to the Infinite,* and *The 8 Laws of Change,* winner of the 2016 Nautilus Book Award for Social Change. *The Vision* is his second novel, the first being *Awakening – A Novel of Aliens and Consciousness* a 2018 winner of the Book Excellence Award for Literary Excellence